Tess's gift had never connected her to a killer before, and she feared she wouldn't survive his game of hide-and-seek . . .

Tess had somehow become Julie, was seeing what Julie saw and feeling what she felt. She looked down at her legs. Her bare flesh was covered with goose bumps. And splattered drops of Jill's blood. Julie was unable to stop the groan that moved through her vocal cords.

"Julie, shut up." The girl next to her let out in a rough, terror-filled whisper.

Slowly, Julie turned and took in the girl next to her. She had short, blond, spiked hair and fierce brown eyes.

"He just killed her, Anna." Julie forced out, and Tess could feel her trying to keep her voice low, but she had very little control left. Her throat was simply too tight. The terror was cold, like claws that dug through her. Julie tried not to cry, but Tess could feel th

"Yeah, like v

before he becom
anymore, but we'
Anna's voice wa
soft.

"I can't. I can't." Now Julie couldn't breathe. Nor could she stop shivering. The next thing Tess heard was screaming. It took several moments to realize the screams came from Julie—and therefore from Tess. "Help! Someone help us! Help! Help us!"

Julie's ch
her, and she s
his face mere
his face. "We
a hike," he sa

His knife
He brought i
amazement, t
wrists to the
said. "I'm sur
to the count

"One. Tw

To: Wayne and Rachel
And Ben and Stephanie
With Love

Other Books by Allie Harrison
No Fear

Coming Soon
Of a Different Breed

Hide and Seek

***

by
Allie Harrison

Hide and Seek
Published by ImaJinn Books

ISBN: 978-1-933417-49-3

10 9 8 7 6 5 4 3 2 1

PUBLISHER'S NOTE:
This book is a work of fiction. Names, characters, places and incidents are products of the author's imagination or are used fictitiously. Any resemblance to actual events or locales or persons, living or dead, is entirely coincidental.

Books are available at quantity discounts when used to promote products or services. For information please write to: Marketing Division, ImaJinn Books, Inc. P.O. Box 74274, Phoenix, AZ, 85087, or call toll free 1-877-625-3592.

Cover design by Patricia Lazarus
Cover credits:
Running girl: adamkaz@istockphoto
Morgue: silavsale@dreamstime

ImaJinn Books, Inc.
P.O. Box 74274, Phoenix, AZ 85087
Toll Free: 1-877-625-3592
http://www.imajinnbooks.com

Chapter One

Grandmama was dead.

Tess Fairmont sucked in a breath and pursed her lips. No one would see her cry. She looked at her own refection in the mirror. "I hate being ten," she said out loud. "My legs look like chicken legs. Rodney Wilkens calls me bunny at school because my teeth are too big. And can I please wear makeup to cover up these ugly freckles. I hate them."

"No, besides your grandmama would not want to see you in makeup. She loved you as you are." There was a pause. Then, "Are you sure you want to go to her funeral?" Lorna, Tess's mother, asked, as she continued braiding Tess's honey-colored hair. "I know you were very close to her, but you don't have to go."

Tess bit her lip for a long moment as she contemplated a way around her mother. "I want to go, Mama. I want to say good-bye. I don't just want to remember her the way she was."

"Tess, it isn't as if she was sick for months. She died suddenly. She looks the same as she did last week. I think it best if you simply remember her that way."

Tess allowed her mother to finish with her hair. "Please, Mama. I need to see her."

Mama let out a heavy breath, and Tess knew she'd get her wish.

Two hours later, she sat between Mama and Daddy. Daddy absently held her hand, and the one time she looked up at him, she thought his usual laughing eyes were sad. Now she stared at her new shoes—black patent leather with a heel. Grandmama had taken her shopping less than three weeks ago and had bought them for her. Would Grandmama have believed her if Tess had told her she'd be wearing them to Grandmama's funeral hardly a month later? Inwardly, Tess smiled. Her grandmama would have laughed and said, "Don't get all dressed up for me, honey. Make it a picnic to celebrate my life and make sure you play ball."

Ever since Grandmama saw Dizzy Dean lead the St. Louis Cardinals to an eight to three win in the first game of the 1934 World Series in Detroit's Navin Field, she was an avid fan. She often confessed to being in love with Dizzy Dean, too.

Tess didn't listen to Father Brannigan. She hoped she wouldn't go to Hell for not listening, but thinking of Grandmama and how much fun she was, and how much fun she made everything else, made Tess's heart feel lighter. And she knew that was what Grandmama would have wanted. She wouldn't want anyone sitting at her funeral with a heavy heart.

But oh, Tess, was going to miss her so much . . .

"Come on, Tess."

Lorna drew Tess's attention with a whisper. Tess looked up and saw it was time to walk closer to the casket, to actually look at Grandmama and to say good-bye. She never wanted to go. But she didn't want to oppose her mother, or leave without saying good-bye, either. She was already worried that a bolt of lightning might zap through the church roof because she'd been daydreaming instead of listening to Father Brannigan, as the nuns taught. Meekly, she followed her mother toward the ornate pink casket. Pink was Grandmama's favorite color.

Before she even drew close, Tess saw her grandmama. Her hair was curled a bit more than usual. And Tess thought the pink on her cheeks looked rather funny with the way it was round. Grandmama would laugh hard if she looked in the mirror.

Tess had never seen a dead person, and she wasn't sure what she'd expected, but this wasn't it. In fact, except for the pink clown cheeks, Tess still thought Grandmama looked as if she were asleep. Tess had, after all, spent many nights with Grandmama and had even shared a bed with her. So Tess knew what she looked like sleeping.

But she wasn't sleeping, and yes, Tess would miss her. She stared down at the dead woman's soft, wrinkled face. How many times had Tess kissed that cheek? How many times had Tess felt those arms hold her close in a warm, healing hug? How many times had Grandmama taken Tess's hand as they crossed the street in front of Grandmama's house, because Grandmama often said no one ever gets too old to need a hand to hold?

Tess would never feel any of those things or hear Grandmama's voice again.

"Can I hold her hand one last time, Mama?" Tess asked.

"Of course."

Without hesitation, Tess reached out and took hold of Grandmama's hand. She was prepared to feel coldness. And she did feel cold, but only for a second before warmth moved up Tess's arm. Then her throat to grew tight. She couldn't breathe. If she didn't know better, she'd think she'd tried to swallow a large marshmallow whole and it was caught in her throat.

Grandmama, her casket, and everyone around Tess disappeared in an instant. Tess saw whiteness, filled with black spots, and recognized it as the ceiling tile in Grandmama's bedroom. Her vision moved to the left, and Tess saw Grandmama's dresser where she kept her jewelry box and loose powder and makeup and her pink hairbrush. In the mirror, she saw Uncle John. He held a pillow in his hands. Tess even smelled Grandmama's perfume she always wore.

Then she heard Uncle John's voice. "I'm tired of waiting for my money, old woman."

Tess felt her own heart pound in her chest, as Uncle John brought the pillow close to her face. Or was it Grandmama's face? She just knew she tried to scream and couldn't, as the cool cotton of the pillowcase filled her world with unending, terrifying darkness. She tried to breathe and couldn't . . .

The next thing Tess heard was screaming—her own.

Her father, gentle and kind but strong, held her wrists and tried to calm her as she kicked and screamed and punched. His dark, wonderful eyes came into focus, and Tess realized she lay on the floor beside Grandmama's casket. Everyone in the room was silent as they stared.

"It was Uncle John," Tess said breathlessly. "He killed Grandmama with a pillow for her money."

The gazes of everyone in the room moved to Uncle John

who stood nearby. After a long moment of hushed silence, several people gasped, and suddenly, Uncle John turned and fled . . .

* * * *

Eighteen years later . . .

The horrid dream of Uncle John staring at her with red, hate-filled eyes was whisked away by the shrill sound of her cell phone. Still half asleep and on automatic pilot, she grasped the small device, opened it and held it to her ear. "Yeah?"

"I've got a body for you, Tess," said a familiar voice.

"Yeah?" Tess glanced at the bedside clock and worked to focus on the numbers. One-thirty-eight. It was times like this that she hated being on call for the Chicago Police Department.

"I'll have her at the morgue for you by the time you get there."

He hung up without a good-bye or an *adios, amigo*, but what Tess hated about Detective Jake Williams was not his lack of greeting or salutations. It was the fact that he referred to the body as a "her." If he'd called the body an "it," it wouldn't be so personal. In fact, she wouldn't have to think of it as a person at all. "Her" made the body a real person—a real *dead* person—a female, a girl or a woman. She would have blond, red, brown, gray, black, or any shade of hair in between. She would be someone's daughter, sister, wife, mother, friend, or lover.

Tess slid her feet to the floor and forced herself into a sitting position, fighting the slight dizziness and clouds that still fogged her mind. She rubbed her eyes and reached for her shirt at the same time.

There was no way she'd ever thank Detective Jake Williams for calling her in the middle of the night, but there were two consolations. One, his call had ended the nightmare that plagued her all too often. And two, at the morgue, she'd get to see Dr. Michael Adams.

Why did she even think about Michael Adams? Why would she allow herself to wonder about him? It was, after all, a waste of time. He was smart, handsome, compassionate—at least to the dead. Why would she ever think he would be the least bit interested in a freak like her?

* * * *

Michael knew Tess was in the room. He didn't have to open his eyes. Even with the absence of perfume, he sensed her. Her own unique woman-scent, over the clean smell of vanilla and some sort of flowery soap, touched him with familiarity and filled him with warmth like sunshine on a perfect spring day.

Wanting nothing more than to breathe her in, he still didn't open his eyes as he leaned back in his chair and kept his legs crossed up on his desk. He thought if he remained quiet, allowing her to think him resting, she might draw closer. He knew she kept her distance, even from him, despite the fact that he never gave her reason to.

Finally, he could put it off no longer. "Hello, Tess," he said.

"Hi, Dr. Adams."

He liked the sound of her voice too, had from the first moment he met her. Throaty and rich, rather deep for a woman, he thought she could make a mint on the radio or perhaps as one of those telephone sex voices men called, paying with credit cards to listen to nasty words or live out their fantasies.

But he was sure glad she walked into his morgue a few times a week instead.

He still didn't move, still kept his eyes closed. Yet, he knew she wouldn't venture far into his office, nor would she touch him. Touch was different for Tess Fairmont. For her, there was nothing casual about touch. She saw things when she touched people—usually dead people. At least, it was the dead people he knew about. He'd seen her touch the dead many times, as she helped the Chicago PD. He heard what she told Detective Williams, and he knew she saw enough to help Williams catch the bad guys. He didn't understand how she did it, but he respected it and didn't question it. Even more, he respected her. He'd never known her to be wrong in what she saw.

At the same time, he wondered what she saw when she touched live people. But then, he seldom saw her get close enough to touch anyone.

He wished she wasn't afraid to touch *him*.

"How did you know I was here?" she asked in that wonderful voice.

"You aren't the only one who sees things sometimes." He opened his eyes and looked at her.

She'd come into his office far enough to be just across the desk from him. Dressed in jeans and a plain red t-shirt, she wasn't glamorous. But she was a looker. Her wavy hair was the color of dark honey, and it was pulled back in a simple ponytail. The deep blue of her eyes seemed to cross the desk and grab him. Her full lips invited him to kiss her.

He longed to release her hair from the barrette that held it and run his fingers through it. While she touched him.

Why did he want her touch so much?

Because he knew she never touched anyone freely. Like a child told he could never have a piece of candy, he craved it, knew it would taste wonderful when it finally reached his tongue.

He vowed then and there that he would feel her touch. And he would feel it soon. "And would you please call me Michael? I think we've known each other long enough to let go of the formalities," he said, deciding that if they were going to be skin to skin soon, they should at least be on a first-name basis.

His question seemed to throw her off balance. For a long moment, she looked down at his desk, as if she couldn't meet his gaze. Michael had no trouble looking at her. She wasn't very tall, five-two, five-three, tops. And curvy. He liked that about her. She had soft-looking hips that he wanted to grasp in his hands as he pressed her against him and . . .

Hell, he was going to have to stop thinking like this, or he'd better stay tucked in his desk chair. Otherwise, when he stood, she might label him just another hard-up guy who fantasizes about sex every three seconds.

Okay, so he did fantasize about sex. But it seemed like these days, he did it when she was either close-by or he thought of her, and he only fantasized about sex with *her*.

And he wished he knew how to get beyond the barricades she always had up. He also wished he could interest her in more than just dead bodies.

"So, tell me about the latest body," she said.

She must be reading his mind. Hell, who was he kidding? She was nothing but business as usual. Cool business, at that. If he didn't find a way to warm her up to him, he was never going to touch her. He was never going to be skin to skin with her. He was never going to move past her barricades and touch her soul. Why would she be interested in some geek who worked with dead bodies more than she did? She probably thought of him as nothing more than a vampire, a man who works in the cold, hidden from the sun with no one to converse with other than the dead.

He had to clear his throat before he spoke. "Female, approximate age late twenties to early thirties."

"Where's Detective Williams?"

"He said he had a lot of paperwork to fill out and he had to meet with some bigwigs."

She seemed to think about that a moment, then said, "He thinks this one is the work of a serial killer, doesn't he?"

He wondered how she'd jumped to that conclusion, but didn't dare ask. "Yes."

"So he's meeting with the FBI, isn't he?"

He noticed something in her eyes. Was it fear? "I think so. If this is the work of a serial killer, the FBI would no doubt be involved. Does that bother you?" It was clear to him that it did. He wished she'd open up and share her fears with him. He'd listen. He wouldn't even force her to get close to him or to touch him.

Unfortunately, she didn't share her thoughts. He had so hoped today would be different—that she would let him see inside, perhaps just a glimmer of the mystery she kept hidden from the world. He wanted to know her. He wanted . . .

Let it go, he thought. *Let her go. It's obvious she's not interested.*

"Why should it bother me?" she asked.

Because you suddenly look as if I'm a pirate making

you walk the plank and sharks are waiting for you in the water, that's why, he thought. He shrugged, as if it didn't matter. Michael unfolded himself from his desk chair and stood. He stretched to ease the stiffness in his shoulders.

"You look tired."

"It's two in the morning." As if he needed to remind her. "And two cars full of teenagers hit head-on yesterday afternoon. It's been a busy night."

"I'm sorry."

"So am I." He led her to the door of his office and headed down to the cooler where the bodies were kept. Without a sound, she followed him.

At the swinging double doors that led into the cooler, he paused, his elbow against the door ready to push his way through. He turned back and met her gaze. "When we're through here, would you care to have a cup of coffee with me?"

Okay, so he wasn't quite ready to give up on her yet, even if she had turned down every offer he'd made for them to have a cup of coffee together.

This time was no different. "No, thank you." Her soft voice echoed off the tiled walls around them. Without another a word, she stepped ahead of him and moved into the cooler.

Just as smoothly, he reached out and grasped her arm, stopping her in mid-step. She turned and looked at him, her expression startled, as if his touch burned her. It was nearly enough to make him let go. He didn't. "Will you ever say yes?"

"No."

She stood just inside the room, and he didn't release her. They stood that way for a long, silent moment, then he said, "You don't like me because I'm a pathologist, stuck down in a cold cellar where I cut on dead people, right?" He should be too tired to care why she always turned him down, but he wasn't. She was the first woman to interest him in a very long time, and he never gave up without a fight. But, hell, as hard as she made it to move forward with her, he could have been a dentist trying to pull her teeth.

She blinked at him, as if she didn't understand the question.

Or perhaps she didn't have an answer. Then she blinked a second time. He stared back, feeling mesmerized. He could drown in her gorgeous blue eyes.

"Which body is it?" she asked, ignoring his question. Her voice sounded deeper, perhaps even rougher, and definitely breathier than usual.

He was just offering a simple cup of coffee, so why did he feel as if she'd just kicked him in the balls? She was more than a head shorter than he, so why did she seem to have the ability to look down at him? He fought the urge to maintain the grip on her arm, to force answers from her. In the end, he let her slip from his grasp. "This one over here."

Because seven of the ten metal slabs in the room were covered with sheet-clad bodies, he had to move to the far end of the room. He stopped in front of correct slab, but he didn't remove the sheet.

He met Tess's gaze. "She's been tortured, bound with something thin like plastic or wire, and cut up. She isn't pretty." He always warned her.

Tess stared back at the man evenly. "None of them are ever pretty." They were all dead, devoid of color and warmth, their faces appearing hollow and empty. "But I'm always glad you warn me."

She had no idea why Dr. Michael Adams was a forensics pathologist who preferred caring for the dead and not the living, She had seen the careful, compassionate way he treated the dead and thought his bedside manner would have been wonderful.

And in the last two minutes, she'd felt his touch. There was more than compassion in his hand; there was warmth and caring and unmistakable desire. Her arm still tingled from his touch, and she had to force a swallow through her suddenly tight throat as her entire body instantly craved his heat. Oddly, her lungs were tight when she pulled in a breath. "You care for them, don't you, even though they're dead?"

She wasn't sure why the question popped out. She shouldn't care that he cared. She should just do her job and get the hell out of here. She shouldn't look at him again. He was just a man—probably no different than any other, whose thoughts rarely went beyond getting into her pants.

But she wanted to know his answer, and she wasn't sure why it was so important. Perhaps his offer of coffee was the straw that broke the camel's back. Perhaps she was just tired of always being alone. Maybe a few hours of sex would be better than being alone. Tess swallowed hard but couldn't stop the tingle that moved through her at the idea.

His next words grounded her and wiped away all thoughts of sex. "They're still people. They're still important. Someone has to care for them."

"I know that's true." Tess looked down at the sheet-covered silhouette. She didn't want to do this, but she had to. By touching this woman, she might be able to save someone else's life.

"Do you need me to pull the sheet down, or just move it enough so you can touch the hand?" Michael Adams suddenly asked.

"It helps if I see the face," she replied. She had to lick her lips to bring some moisture to her mouth. She knew that, when it worked, her ability helped Detective Jake Williams, but no one knew how much it took out of her or how sick to her stomach she felt before she put it to the test.

"Let me know when you're ready," Michael said, interrupting her thoughts.

She took a deep breath and exhaled, then said, "I'm ready." As usual, it was a lie. The truth was she was never ready to see them.

Tess forced herself to breathe as Michael pulled back the sheet. She tried to look at the body and not see the woman as a person. She did her best to look past the dark, wavy hair. But the bruises on the delicate lines of her cheeks and the dried blood was impossible to ignore and caused her stomach to twist. She stared at the woman for a long moment, seeing a life violently cut short.

Why this woman? she wondered. *Why this woman when my own life seems to float along with little meaning?*

She suddenly wanted more.

She suddenly wanted to do more than float along.

And the only way her life could get meaning was if she put it out there . . .

"Michael?" It was the first time she'd used his first name, and she said it hesitantly. Her voice sounded loud and seemed to echo off the room's walls, and she didn't look at him. He stood so close that she smelled the clean, man scent of him over the room's smell of death and disinfectant. Her heartbeat quickened. She thought if he touched her now she might jump right out of her skin.

"Yes?" he said.

"I always say no because I don't like coffee," she admitted. She didn't meet his gaze as she spoke, but she felt as if she could read his thoughts. He had to know it was so much more than the fact that she didn't like coffee since they both knew she could get just about anything other than coffee at a coffee shop.

She suddenly felt as though she could taste the bitter tang of coffee, and she swallowed hard. Closing her eyes, she thought, *Not now. I can't think of that now.*

Right then, she had to concentrate on this woman. She had to touch this *person* with her mind clear in order to see anything that might come to her. Without another word and before any further thoughts could creep into her mind, Tess reached out unhesitatingly and took the girl's hand in her own.

As Michael tried to decide how to respond to Tess's sudden revelation about not liking coffee, he watched her lift the girl's hand. He knew from what she'd told him in the past that, at first, she felt nothing but the cold, lifeless touch of death. She'd also told him that if she would be allowed to see anything at all, it would happen fast, after she felt a warmth rush over her. Then she became the victim, and she saw through the victim's eyes whatever the victim had seen in the last moments of life. Tess had never told him much about exactly what she physically or emotionally experienced, but at times, he knew from her expression that she also felt the pain the victim had endured.

Michael waited and watched her, suddenly realizing he held his breath. He wondered how many people knew of Tess's gift—or curse, as she often called it. Besides himself and Jake

Williams, he doubted there were many.

In fact, Tess kept to herself so much that he wondered if she even had friends. He often saw her eating lunch in the diner, but she usually sat in a booth alone. One of these days, he planned to sit in the booth with her.

There he was, back to putting himself close to her. He might as well face facts; she was closer to Detective Jake Williams. He figured Jake, at least, had her phone number, which was more than he had.

And as for Detective Jake Williams, Michael had been in this cool room with him enough to know Jake's heart could be just as cool. Then again, perhaps he'd just seen so many dead bodies that he'd become immune to the sight. Perhaps he could turn off his feelings when he came here to examine one, and perhaps later, when he was alone, he gave in to the pain he certainly must feel when he reflected back on the agony he knew the victims had obviously endured. Yes, Jake could be a cool cucumber, but Michael saw the way he treated Tess with respect even though Tess didn't appear to give Jake the time of day any more than she did him. He supposed he should be grateful for that.

As he continued to watch Tess, Michael thought about the past five weeks. There had been three previous victims, and Detective Williams had called Tess in on all of them. Thus far, she claimed to have received nothing more than fuzzy images when she took the hands of the dead victims. She'd told Michael about blurry, dirty white walls and the moving image of a small, cloudy fish aquarium, none of which could help the police find the killer.

Tess made a sudden movement, and Michael was jerked back to the present. Watching her was difficult, often even more difficult than watching family members grieve when they came into this room to identify their loved ones. At least they didn't actually feel what had happened to that loved one.

And he knew that Tess was feeling something. He saw her stiffen, and her breathing grew shallow. Gooseflesh popped out on her arms, and she shivered uncontrollably. She was suddenly tense. She opened her mouth, and Michael thought she might scream, but only a terror-filled moan managed to escape. He stared at a single drop of blood that dripped from her hand—the free hand that didn't touch the woman. Tess's fist was clenched so tightly, her nails cut into her palm. It took everything he had not to grab her and pull her into his arms. Yet, he didn't dare move closer because he had no idea what touching her at a time like this would do to her.

Tess wasn't aware of Michael's attention. Indeed, she wasn't herself any longer, and she shuddered at the scene surrounding her.

She sat in a straight-back dining room chair. When she tried to move, pain shot up each arm from the raw burns on her wrists that were caused by plastic wire that bound her to the chair's arms. She blinked back tears, looked to her left and saw him—the back of a man in the kitchen. He had dark hair and broad shoulders, no identifying marks. Was there something familiar about him? She wasn't sure.

What frightened her most were the others in the room with her. Five women about her age—twenty-five to perhaps thirty. They were all like her—terrified, tearful, nearly naked, bound to the chairs on which they sat.

Tess tried to study each one carefully, but she was unable to change the past or change anything this victim did in the moments before her death, so she was unable to let her gaze linger on each hostage or on anything about the room unless the victim did.

Then the woman turned her gaze back to the kitchen. "Why are you doing this?" the woman called out. Yes, that was what Tess wanted to know, too.

"I already told you, you're not to speak unless spoken to. Have I not made myself clear?"

He did something in the kitchen, something that made a scraping sound. Scrape up, scrape back, but Tess couldn't place it. He paused in his motion. "Have I not? You'd better answer me."

Tess felt the woman swallow hard. She also felt the woman's desire to defy him. In the end, the victim said, "Yes, you have. I'm sorry, I still don't understand why. Why me?"

Tess had a million other questions she wanted to ask, and was frustrated that she only saw and did whatever the victim had seen and done.

The scraping sound continued. It raked on every nerve in her body like nails on a chalkboard. Then it stopped. Above the soft sobs of the woman in the chair next to her, Tess heard her own heart pounding. He turned to her slightly, just enough to show his profile. He had a handsome face and a dimple in his right cheek appeared as he smiled at her.

"You're all guilty of a crime. And now it's time for your sentence to be handed down."

She stared at him, working to place his face. "What crime, Raymond?" the victim asked. "I didn't do anything to you."

Good question. And Raymond? Tess felt a small thrill of excitement She knows his name, at least his first name.

"That's exactly right, you didn't do anything. But if you can't remember your crime completely, I'm sure you'll be reminded of it in Hell."

Tess felt she should know more than just his first name, more than if he'd simply told the woman his name was Raymond. He stepped forward, and Tess wanted to scream with frustration because as he moved closer, showing his full profile, the victim did not look at his face.

Then Tess was hit with a soul-deep cold as the victim's gaze moved to what he held in his hand. A knife, large, gleaming and sharp as a razor. That's what the scraping sound had been—he'd been sharpening the knife. She tried to swallow and couldn't.

"Please don't do this." The woman's whispered words burned in Tess's throat.

Tess knew she couldn't stop him, knew she couldn't change what already was. Still, she struggled against the bonds at her wrists, ignoring the pain they caused. Her nails bit into the arms of the chair.

The knife came toward her. When more pain came, she

screamed and screamed and screamed . . .

* * * *

Tess felt herself falling and couldn't stop. Then there was only darkness.

She woke to find herself looking up at Michael. It took a long moment for her to gather her wits. When she finally managed it, she discovered she was in Michael's arms and he held her on his lap. A quick glance around told her they were on the small sofa in the hallway outside the cooler.

She tried to jump away from him, but didn't manage anything more than almost falling off the sofa.

"Whoa." He kept her from falling and shifted her closer to him.

His touch was everywhere. Warmth, heat, and an electrical current, something like touching her tongue to a nine-volt battery, buzzed through her. She shifted in his arms slightly. Her movement didn't stop the current.

"No, don't try to move. Just breathe, nice and easy," he instructed.

Easy for him to say when all she really wanted to do was melt against him. His closeness was like warm, inviting water flowing around her, flowing through her. She suddenly wanted nothing more than to swim against him.

"What happened?" She had to force those two words out through a still painfully tight throat.

"You screamed, then fainted. I managed to keep you from hitting the floor. I didn't think you'd appreciate waking up on a slab with the bodies in there, so I brought you out here."

The concern she saw etched in his expression melted the cold spot in her soul. And his touch was so warm, so vibrant. Along with the current and the warmth of water against her, a bright blue light surrounded him. She had to close her eyes against it for a long moment.

"What did you see when you touched that woman?" he asked.

She didn't answer but merely looked down at herself to make sure there were no holes in her clothes, no blood pouring from wounds.

She was intact, whole. And her only pain was in her chest where her heart beat wildly enough to hurt, but whether her heart raced because of what she'd just seen or because she was in Michael's arms, or perhaps a combination of the two, Tess wasn't sure. She started to sit up, but couldn't. So she remained leaning against him. His hands were so strong, so gentle. He held her as if she were a precious piece of glass he was afraid he'd break.

"Easy," Michael said. "Are you feeling up to talking about what you saw?"

She wasn't feeling up to it, never would be, but she had to do it anyway. "He . . . he . . " It was impossible to speak as she gasped for breath, feeling as if she'd just sprinted a mile.

"It's all right. I know what he did to her. You don't have to think about that part. Just concentrate on the part that will help Detective Williams find him and stop him before he hurts another woman."

"This time was so different," she said, still out of breath, her words shaky as the fear slowly dissipated.

"How was it different?"

She shook her head as she searched for the right words to describe her experience. "It wasn't just a flash or a moment of bits and pieces, as it usually is. It was vivid and real, like dropping into the middle of a movie. I saw him—his profile, I mean. He seemed so familiar, and *she* knew him." Tess met Michael's warm, concerned gaze. "And what's worse is that he plans to hurt other women. I saw five of them, all tied up just as I was. I mean just as *she* was."

"As soon as we get upstairs, I'll call Detective Williams. How do you feel?"

"I think I'll be all right," she lied. With all the effort she could muster, she moved off his lap and worked to sit up next to him without having to lean on him like a crutch. She tried to stand and weaved slightly, and she found herself wanting to reach out to him, to touch him.

She frowned, confused. She shouldn't want his touch, shouldn't need it. She didn't *want* to need it or to want it in any way. Yet, it was as if her body leaned toward him without any command from her brain. When he placed an arm around her waist to steady her, Tess let him.

She admitted to herself that his touch was not like anyone else's. He was not a hormone-controlled teenager. He'd held her in his arms, and yet, he didn't act like a man who planned to put his hands where she didn't want them. Even now, she felt mere concern in his touch. Why had she ever feared his touch? It was warm, secure, and safe. In his touch, she felt trust, as if that current in him moved from his hands and into her soul. She could be sure about him. In his hands, she felt pure goodness and gentleness.

Still, she shouldn't want his touch. She'd learned long ago that touch often led to pain—pain she didn't want and pain she didn't think she could handle. She'd rather never again feel someone's touch than to feel that pain. Still, she didn't pull away as he led her toward the stairs, and he never let go of her.

When they reached the top of the stairs, she said, "My legs feel so heavy, so weak. I can't believe how drained this has left me. It's as if the woman's terror sucked out every once of my energy."

"Have you ever felt that way before?" He pulled her closer against him and steered her into his office where he led her to an old sofa he had stashed in there.

"Yes, but not this much. And—"

"And what?"

"And usually after I touch someone and have a vision, I have a headache," she answered. *That was putting it mildly. Sometimes a mere flash of vision could make her head feel as though someone had put an ice pick in it.* "Tell me what else happened," she said. "Did I say anything?"

"No, I already told you. You flinched as if you were in pain and moaned, and then you started screaming."

"That was because I felt him stick her with that knife."

She'd spoken without thinking, but if it shocked him, he didn't show it. His voice was cool and professional as he asked, "Have you ever felt that before?"

She absently rubbed her face and took a deep breath. But

when she closed her eyes, she saw the scene again—his next victims; his hideous smile. "I usually feel the victim's emotions, not so much physical pain. I don't remember ever feeling anything as strong as this. But then, I'm not sure any of my visions have ever been this vivid, either." She sighed. "Why do I do this to myself?"

"To help people. Here, take this."

She looked up to find he held a mug out to her.

He smiled. "It's not coffee, I promise. It's just water. It's all I have right now."

She took it from him. Her fingers brushed his, and even though it had been just minutes since she'd felt his warmth, the heat of him startled her. It didn't burn, like the sudden touch of a match. It was more like she'd been out in the cold darkness for a long time and now drew close to an inviting fire. It made her want to turn so that each part of her body could experience the warmth, too.

Her hand shook, and she was forced to hold the glass with both hands. But she took a drink and let the water's coolness wash through her raw throat. She sat quietly while he moved to his desk and picked up his phone. She felt suddenly cold and fought down a shiver at the loss of the fire that was Michael. And yet she still saw the deep outline of his blue aura around him—his clean blue, warm and pure aura. It shimmered to blue-green at times as she watched. Why had she never seen that before? Probably because he'd never touched her before.

"You saw him?" he asked her as he dialed.

"Yes, his profile, and his other intended victims, all bound to chairs, too. I also saw that same cloudy fish tank that I'd seen during my previous visions. Detective Williams is right. He does have a serial killer. And today's victim knew his name."

"His name?"

"I—I mean she called him Raymond."

Michael swore under his breath, then he spoke into the phone. "Detective Williams? This is Michael Adams. Yes, Tess is here, and I think you'd better get back here as soon as possible. You should probably bring one of your police artists, too."

Chapter Two

At six-foot-four, he towered over Tess with more than a foot to spare. Yet, Dr. Michael Adams never looked down at her. Why hadn't she ever noticed that? In the past two hours, there was a lot she had never noticed that she now saw. It was probably due to the fact that she'd never touched him before.

Nor had she ever been in his arms. She'd forgotten how warm real touch was. And his was exceptionally warm.

She waited for pain, the usual headache, but none came. Give it time, she thought.

She sat in his office finishing with Marilyn, the best police artist she'd ever been given the chance to work with. The details and the way Marilyn brought back memories were amazing. The profile she drew of the killer with dark hair was frighteningly perfect.

Michael leaned over her left shoulder and looked at the sketch. Tess glanced sideways at him. He still wore his white lab coat, and in his blue eyes, Tess saw signs of fatigue. His dark blond hair fell haphazardly down into his eyes, and he absently raked his fingers through it to set it back in place. "So you really feel you should know him?"

Tess shook her head slightly. "I don't know." She waited until Marilyn stepped away, taking the sketch with her to make copies before she continued. "In the vision, he seemed familiar, but perhaps I was only feeling fragments of the victim's feelings since she knew him well enough to call him Raymond, because now that I look at him, he doesn't look familiar at all."

Jake Williams stepped into the room. "We'll distribute this sketch as soon as possible. And we'll see if the computer can match anything to the name Raymond. Is there anything else you can add, anything else you remember?"

Tess had described the room, complete with the dirty walls and small fish tank from her past visions, and all of the five other women as she remembered them. She even described the killer's voice and the way he moved. "No, if I think of anything else, I'll call you, Detective Williams." She rubbed her forehead absently, feeling too tired to remember another memory of anything.

Jake looked at her squarely. "Call me Jake."

Tess nodded slowly. Twice now, like a small child, she'd been given permission to move to another plane.

"You know I have to give a report to the FBI," he told her.

"I know."

"What do you want me to tell them—that I got this information from a psychic?"

Tess took a deep breath and absently scratched her head. Her entire past was filled with being shunned because everyone thought she was "different." During her growing up years, people labeled her as witch, psychic or psycho, weird or strange. It didn't matter. Regardless of the label, they were afraid to touch her. She had the feeling that the moment word of her ability got out now, she'd experience that all over again, at least from most people. Until now, Jake Williams had managed to use her ability and blend it with other evidence to protect her. Perhaps this was where the pain would come in—from being ostracized by the few people she'd befriended here.

When the memory came back of what the woman lying on a slab in the cooler had gone through at the hands of this monster, it suddenly didn't matter any longer. It didn't matter if anyone knew of her "gift." It didn't matter if there was pain. All that mattered was saving those other five women. "I don't care what you tell them."

"I'll tell them it came from an unidentified informant and see how that flies, but don't expect any miracles. They brought with them three other unsolved cases from the past year, from other parts of the country. Every case matches the profile of these recent murders. It looks like our man's a busy guy, especially if he's got five more waiting for her turn." Jake took a deep breath and let it out slowly. "I'll be in touch."

"Good night, Jake," Michael said.

"I can hope for a good night, can't I?" Jake left, walking out with a heavy tread, as if he were tired and much older than his thirty-something years.

A moment later, Tess was alone with Michael. For a full minute, the room was perfectly quiet. Tess lowered her head and closed her eyes, letting her body relax. Forcing herself to relive the vision over and over in order to grasp every detail for Jake and the police artist had left her feeling beaten.

"Why don't you let me drive you home?"

Michael's offer touched her with almost the same warmth his hands offered. And Tess couldn't help smiling. "What about my car?"

"We can leave it here, and I can pick you up and bring you back whenever you're ready to come get it."

"I couldn't impose on you like that. I'm sure you'll have to go out of your way to take me home, and you look exhausted. You need to go home to bed."

"I'm used to long hours," he said, as he looked at his watch. "Besides, as of one hour ago, when Riley showed up for the next shift, I was officially off duty for a week, so I have plenty of time to catch up on my sleep."

"Taking a vacation, are you?"

He grinned at her. "My boss told me I needed to use up some of my accumulated vacation time or I was going to lose it. I plan on stopping for breakfast before heading home. Care to join me? I promise I won't force any coffee on you."

Tess smiled again. She also recalled his touch. There was no denying his warmth, his goodness. Nor could she deny the clean, blue aura she saw around him, as well as the clean aura that was left on everything he touched. She wondered why she'd never seen it until he touched her.

Best of all, there was no pain, no headache. Perhaps there wouldn't be. Tess found herself wishing for that.

She must have hesitated too long before replying, for he went on, "Or if you don't care to hit the diner across the street, we could go to my place. It's not too far and I make a mean omelet."

The grin he offered her played across her heartstrings like the bow of a fine violin. She didn't want to leave. She didn't want to go home yet. After feeling his touch, she found she couldn't just walk away. Not now, perhaps not ever, but she couldn't let herself think about that when the horror of her previous vision was so fresh and raw. No matter how much she thought spending time with him wasn't a good idea, her desire to do just that won over. He'd helped her and held her after one of the worst visions she'd ever experienced, and the last thing she wanted right now was to face the rest of the world or her empty house alone.

His place would be better, she knew from past experience. At the diner, she'd be bombarded by feelings left by previous patrons where something as simple as touching the salt shaker could give her headache behind her eyes.

What really made up her mind was the fact that she was starving. Breakfast sounded like a great idea. Her stomach growled with anticipation. "Your omelet sounds great. I'll be happy to join you for breakfast, but I can drive myself." She didn't add that she wanted to drive herself so she could leave if any feelings she experienced at his house were too much for her to handle. A shiver passed through her. She knew without a doubt that any feelings regarding Michael might grew into something more. Maybe that was what she wanted . . .

Thirty minutes later, after following him in her own car, Tess was in his home. Talk about jumping in with both feet, she thought wryly, as she stood on the far side of the kitchen island and watched him move around as if he cooked gourmet breakfasts every morning.

Michael couldn't believe Tess was in his kitchen. He had clearly seen the tug of war in her eyes when he'd asked her to come home and have breakfast with him. But then, since she'd awakened in his arms, he'd seen that tug of war in her expression more than once when she looked at him. He was beginning to wonder what the hell she'd "seen" when she woke in his arms and had tried to jump away from him. He decided it didn't really matter. She was here with him, and that's what he'd wanted.

"Sausage with my killer omelet?" he offered, opening the fridge.

"That'd be great," she replied.

He heard the anxiety in her voice and wished he could put

her at ease. "Pancakes, English muffins, or bagels?"

He stood up and met her gaze. She looked like a deer surrounded by wolves.

"Whatever you want."

He didn't look away. Enough was enough. He couldn't let her spend the entire meal being afraid of him. "You're nervous," he pointed out. "You don't have to be nervous in my house."

She licked her lips, and he couldn't help staring at the motion of her tongue. Maybe he should look back into the fridge. Maybe he should climb into the fridge and cool off. He still didn't look away from her.

"You really know how to read me, don't you?"

He shrugged. "I'd like to," he replied honestly, knowing instinctively that it was the only way to deal with her.

"You don't understand. I'm not used to spending time in anyone else's kitchen."

"I noticed the way you haven't moved an inch since we arrived, and you've been careful to not even touch the counter." He paused. "Tess, you can touch things here. I'm not afraid of your touch, and you don't have to be afraid of mine. I don't have anything to hide. And if it makes you feel any better, I'm not used to having anyone in my kitchen for breakfast, either."

She offered him a small smile.

"Now, what is it—pancakes, English muffins, or bagels? Or do you want all three?"

She laughed, even if it did sound a bit forced. "Only if I want to wind up fat as a pig. I think I'll just have the English muffin."

"Great." He pulled out a tray of eggs and the package of sausage, then moved to another cabinet to get out the toaster.

"Do you always eat this much for breakfast?" she asked.

"Breakfast is the most important meal of the day, you know."

"Well, just don't expect to find all that in my refrigerator."

"And what will I find in your refrigerator?" he asked, taking it as subtle invitation that he would soon get to spend time in her kitchen.

"Skim milk, orange juice, maybe some eggs, but I wouldn't

trust eating them. They may be petrified."

He shared her grin as he pulled out a pitcher and a can of juice concentrate and slid them both over the counter to her. "Would you care to mix the juice?"

"Sure."

He couldn't mistake the hesitancy in her voice, and he wished for a way to help her relax.

The smell and sizzling sounds of cooking pork filled the room within moments.

"I understand what you see when you take the hands of the dead," Michael said without turning toward her, pretending he was too busy poking the sausage with a fork. He sensed that it would be easier for her to talk if he wasn't looking at her. "But what do you see when you touch other objects?"

"It's hard to explain. I don't really see anything. I just feel. And it's only sometimes, not all the time." She zipped the lid off the juice.

"Like what?"

"Like a feeling of goodness or badness or uncleanliness."

"You're right, I can see where that's hard to explain since I don't really understand what that would feel like." He risked a glance at her. "Can you expound on that a little?"

She shrugged lightly. "It's like a few weeks ago. I was in the diner eating lunch. I like being in the diner. I can have a great meal and still be around people."

It tore at him know her worry ran that deep, but he said nothing, wanting her to keep talking. "Anyway, when I picked up the salt shaker to salt my potato, I felt the lingering feeling of dirtiness, like an illness. I know that sounds funny, but I'm almost positive the person who held it last is probably sick with something like cancer or in the end stages of some other disease. Usually, I feel nothing. The vibes, or whatever they are that I feel, have to be very strong. That's why I usually feel things like extreme happiness or extreme excitement or like with this serial killer, extreme evil. And the most frustrating part is that I don't feel it all the time."

"Why's that the most frustrating part?"

"Because it's like anticipating something all the time and it only shows up half the time, so you can never relax because you never know if this will be the time. Does that make sense?"

"Absolutely." He pulled out a plate and covered it with a paper towel for the cooked pork. "So why don't you like the FBI?"

He asked his question with his back to her as he cooked because he again felt she'd be more open with him if she wasn't being watched.

"I never said I didn't like the FBI."

He looked at her over his shoulder. "You didn't have to. It was written in your expression when you said those three initials. If you'd like to have a glass of that juice before we eat, glasses are in that cabinet right there." He nodded toward a nearby cabinet.

"Would you care for some, too?" she asked.

"Yes, please."

It must be getting easier for her to touch his things, he thought, as he watched her out of the corner of his eye. He saw no hesitation when she opened the cabinet and reached in for two glasses. She also got out two plates and set the small table.

He also knew his request for juice gave her an opportunity to ignore his question about the FBI which was why he was surprised when she went on with, "I don't have a problem with the FBI—just one agent."

He couldn't believe she'd just admitted that to him. And those three words brought up so many questions—which agent? Why? What happened? Michael fought the urge to blurt them all out, wishing she trusted him enough to share this with him. He wished, too, that he knew how to put her at ease. She was obviously so surprised she'd let her thoughts slip that she looked like a deer caught in the headlights.

Tess's heart suddenly raced. She couldn't believe she'd even allowed herself to think about Markus Black, much less mention him. She'd thought she'd managed to tuck him so far back behind the locked doors of her mind that he could never escape.

"I see," Michael said absently.

Tess knew there was nothing for him to see. Yet, it was as if Markus Black was suddenly in the room with them. He filled the room with his filth. Tess even smelled him—that horrid mixture of aftershave and man and a strong deodorant that tried to mask the other smells and couldn't. There was even an underlying hint of the coffee he'd bought for her. For a moment, she actually tasted bitterness and thought she might throw up, but there was nothing in her stomach. Still, she nearly heaved.

From far away, she heard Michael's voice. "Tess?"

She took a deep breath and looked at him, wondering just when he'd crossed the room and touched her arm. His hand on her arm was . . .

Inviting.

Pleasing.

Alluring.

Safe.

And not the least bit painful.

"Are you all right?"

Tess couldn't respond to his question. Why was she reacting this way to the memory of Markus Black? And why now? It had been nearly four years. She'd long ago moved on with her life and left the horrid memories of Markus Black at the side of the road.

Then she realized what was making her react this way..

"It was the smell," she said out loud, forcing the words through her tight throat.

"What smell? The sausage?"

"No! That smells good." In all reality, Markus Black smelled good, too—alluring. It had been what drew her to him. It had been discovering later just how rotten he was inside that turned his scent vile. "I just remembered the smell of the killer's house. I need to call Jake and tell him."

"You *smelled* his house?"

Tess took slow, even breaths and worked to clear away the memory. "Yes, now that I think about it, everything in that vision was exceptionally vivid—the smell, the feel of the wood of the chair arms where my, I mean *her*, hands were bound. I even had goose bumps because I was sitting there in nothing more than my underwear and the house was cool. It was the strongest vision I've ever had."

The sausage began to burn, and even though they both glanced toward the stove, Michael didn't leave her side. "What did his house smell like?"

"Like a locker room—musty and sweaty, like dirty socks with air freshener working to cover it up. Our breakfast is burning."

For a long moment, they remained still. Close enough that Tess again smelled the clean, pure, enticing scent of him; close enough that she felt the heat of his body. She instinctively felt the urge to move away, to create some space, but she didn't give into that urge. She didn't move at all. After all, his touch, his smell, his very closeness, was nice, inviting, as it wiped away the remnants of her locker room memory.

Michael didn't move his hand from her arm for a long moment. Then, as if he feared he'd invaded too much of her space, he suddenly stepped away and pointed to the phone next to his computer. "The phone is over there."

Tess was still hesitant to move away from him. Yes, closeness was frightening to her, but at the same time, Michael came with a safe feeling. With him, Tess didn't see or feel the coldness she felt from so many other people. Was it really possible he accepted her, gift and all, when all her life she'd been abandoned to the wolves? Tess was afraid to hope, despite how she was drawn to the warmth Michael offered. Finally, she forced her legs to move, and she headed to the desk where she made the call and reported her memory to Jake.

Yet, for her, breakfast was ruined after she made the call. Try as she might, she couldn't seem to bury memories of Markus Black. They lingered, along with the memories of her vision and the haunting odor of a locker room.

Much to her surprise, Michael was observant enough to notice her lack of appetite because he said, "You aren't eating."

"I'm not as hungry as I thought I was."

"Why not? Was it because you remembered the smell or the feel of the chair?" He'd polite enough to wait until they were both finished eating before he brought up the subject. "Or did it have more to do with the one FBI agent you don't like?"

For a long moment, Tess stared at her nearly empty plate. "I know they say one bad apple doesn't make all the apples in the bucket bad. But for me, I find it hard to work with any of them knowing they hire men like him."

"Men like whom?"

She shook her head. In Michael's line of work, he dealt with many law enforcement people. Chances were he knew Markus Black. "I shouldn't say, and it's not important anyway. Unless they find another body, I probably won't meet up with him. Besides, he probably won't even be one of the agents assigned to the case. And if he is, well, I'm a big girl and I know how to remain professional. I should have never brought him up. I guess I'm more tired than I thought."

She offered him a small smile, knowing it wasn't anything close to an explanation, but right then she was too tired to give any more. She was relieved when he returned her smile.

She helped him wash dishes, then insisted she had to go. They both needed sleep. Despite the fact he had the next week off, they both knew there were five potential victims that could show up on the slabs in his cooler. She suspected he'd cancel his vacation if that started happening. And her vision had wiped her out. If she didn't get some sleep soon, she'd collapse right where she stood.

Michael walked her to her car. The world was waking up to a perfect, early spring morning, complete with a pink sky. The neighborhood was quiet as the sun peeked over the housetops. Somewhere down the street, an early worker slammed a car door.

"Thanks for sharing breakfast with me," he said.

"It was fun. Thanks for not forcing any coffee on me."

He rolled his eyes. He knew it wasn't as fun as it could have been had she not had to call Jake Williams with more information about her vision. "Now that I know you don't like it, I won't offer it again." He reached out and took her hand. "What about hot chocolate or tea, do you like those?"

She smiled and let him hold her hand, enjoying the leathered softness of his skin and the warmth it infused in her. She wondered what he'd say if she told him that when he held her hand, she'd do whatever he wanted. "Yes, I like both."

"If you like, we could do something this week while I'm off. If the sun stays out, maybe we could go on a picnic or something," he suggested.

She concentrated on his hand in hers and still didn't sense any coldness or anything that felt dirty or distrustful. More importantly, there was no pain. She was afraid of the pain. But she decided to take the chance. "I'd like that."

"If the sun doesn't stay out, we could take in a movie. Do you like butter on your popcorn?"

"Of course, extra. But if it's all right with you, I'd rather just rent a movie. Movie theatres are too . . . full of people"

"I get it," he said. "We can rent something and I'll make the popcorn."

She watched him for a long moment. "Do you know you're surrounded by a blue-green aura?"

He raised his brows at her question. "Is that good?"

"Yes, it's very good." And something she wanted to trust.

Without another word, or without giving her warning, he leaned close and tenderly touched his lips to hers. The kiss was quick but soft, over in the span of a heartbeat. Yet, her heart fluttered as if it was filled with a million butterflies.

She stared up at him for a long moment, surprised— surprised that he'd kissed her and surprised by her own reaction to his kiss. She fought the urge to lick her lips, not wanting to lick away the lingering taste of him or the way her lips tingled from his contact. Long ago, thanks to Markus Black, she'd given up the idea of ever kissing anyone again.

But with Michael, every cell of her being was suddenly alive, awake, and alert. And craving more. She was instantly reminded how wonderfully good flesh against flesh could feel.

Yet, he apparently mistook her surprise for anger, because he said, "I won't say I'm sorry for that kiss, Tess, because I'm not. And don't try to convince me you didn't like it. It may have been quick, but I felt the way you responded."

"All right, I won't try to convince you. And I'm glad you're not sorry, because I'm not, either. But I do have a question. Why are you working with dead people? You should be a medical doctor, healing and saving patients' lives."

He gave her a small grin and shook his head. "That life isn't for me. I'm right where I need to be." He opened her car door for her. "Why are you working with dead people? With your voice, you could choose to be on any radio show you wanted."

"You're kidding, right?"

He merely grinned at her. "Can I call you later?"

"Okay." She was startled by how quickly she'd agreed. She was doing more than taking chances with him. She was not only jumping into the pool with both feet, but into water that was probably over her head. She climbed in behind the wheel. They said good-bye, and she drove off, refusing to watch him in the rearview mirror.

As Michael watched Tess go, he thought about her suggestion that he should be treating live patients. He could never be a practicing physician. He couldn't heal the sick. That's why it was best he simply cared for the dead. Emma had taught him that.

Emma.

For the first time in four years, his heart didn't ache at the thought of her. He wondered what Tess would say if he told her that he needed her touch as much as she needed his.

* * * *

Tess's lips still tingled, and she felt Michael's warmth rolling through her for the entire drive south, out of Chicago. Not until she pulled to a stop in her own garage in the small village suburb of Willow did she hesitantly lick her lips. Her heart skipped a beat when she still tasted Michael.

She climbed out and looked around at the familiarity of her neighborhood. Named for a small grove of weeping willow trees that had grown wild a century before, Willow seldom changed. It maintained its own public schools, had four churches and three gas stations, as well as five bars and a small grocery store. Yet, unlike the ever-changing windy city of Chicago,

Willow's population stayed relatively the same.

Tess lived in a bungalow at the corner of First Street and Chestnut. She had a waving acquaintance with her neighbors, but never got close enough to have to touch them. She maintained her yard and house and lived among the residents as if she were one of them, which she knew she never would be. Despite the charade, she'd made a quiet life for herself. She was on the payroll of the Chicago Police Department, under Detective Jake Williams' supervision, leaving behind a childhood of being shunned and called names while doing her best to keep her chin up and ignore the taunts.

Now, as she looked at the little stone house she'd grown to love, her lips still tingled. Tentatively, she reached up and gently fingered them, as if she might actually still feel the remnants of Michael's lips. Could she trust this? Could she trust him and the goodness she felt in him?

She'd walked into his cooler over two years ago, and he'd never treated her with anything other than respect, even after witnessing her "gift" in action. Did that mean he was trustworthy?

It had been four years since that single night with Markus Black reminded her that sometimes the taunts of school children simply grow into something bigger, something worse. It had been four long years since she'd smelled that expensive aftershave scent she knew he used to mask his rotten soul. And yet her vision about the killer's house had brought it all back in an instant, and just when she was beginning to feel almost comfortable in Michael's kitchen, too. Why had it had to surface then?

Would she have not been lured in so easily by Markus Black if she had never gone to Grandmama's funeral? How different would her life be if she had just walked past Grandmama's casket without taking her hand and discovering her 'gift' before her entire family? Would she have grown up with friends instead of being called a freak, or a weirdo, or a witch, or psychotic? Would she have had the self-esteem to recognize Markus Black for the user he was? Perhaps. Would she perhaps have a husband—a husband who was nice and good-looking like Michael Adams,? And would there be kids playing in this yard and filling the two empty bedrooms of her house?

As she asked herself those questions, her lips still tingled from Michael's kiss.

That tingle scared the hell out of her. That tingle sent a buzz through her that caused her insides to shake and make all of her feel antsy and needy and lonelier than ever because it was making her want to dream of a home and a family. It was making her want a life she knew she could never have.

But then again, Michael filled her with warmth, and she'd seen nothing but goodness when his lips touched hers. Dare she hope for more?

* * * *

Michael made his way to his bedroom, thinking how empty and lifeless the house felt now that Tess was gone. It was a feeling he hadn't experienced since Emma.

When he stepped into his bedroom, he walked to his chest of drawers where he kept one last photograph of Emma on display. He had snapped the picture of her the summer before she'd gotten sick, the summer before he'd discovered the lump in her breast, the summer before the radical mastectomy and all the radiation that did nothing to stop the disease that coursed through her.

Lifting the framed photo, he walked to his mattress and flopped down onto his bed. Holding the picture above him, he looked up at Emma, his wife of ten short months. He could almost imagine her long blond hair cascading down toward him. In her smile, he saw her openness. She'd been bubbly and outgoing, beautiful and quick to laugh. There'd been no mystery to her. He'd never had to wonder what she thought. She'd shared everything with him and wore her heart and emotions on her sleeve for the entire world to see and love.

He'd loved her completely, would have done anything for her. But he hadn't been able heal her.

It was when Emma died in his arms that he made his decision to care for the dead. He had nearly gone crazy with wonder as to what was done with her after she was taken from her hospital bed for the last time. Did anyone care if she slid off the stretcher and hit the floor? Did anyone think she felt any pain? Did anyone care if she was naked and cold on a cold table in a cold room for anyone to see?

He'd cared, and he'd realized that the dead needed as much, if not more, care than those who lived because they could no longer be their own advocate.

After Emma's death, he'd spent time in what he called limbo. Now he devoted his life to his work, taking care of the dead, especially for those who died for no apparent reason. He searched for answers, for the missing puzzle pieces, to give to the families regarding why and how their loved ones died and to give to the police so they could catch the criminals who cut someone's life short. The dead had so much to tell, and Michael took the time to listen. At the same time, he cared for them as he had wanted Emma cared for. He maintained their dignity. He made sure none of them landed on the floor. He kept them covered, even though they needed to be kept cool.

The dead often held many secrets, but they couldn't speak so they couldn't share them with him. Over the years, he'd learned where to find those secrets, and he'd made it his life's work to speak for them.

And Emma, who had shared so little time with him in her life, had, in her death, taught him to care, to listen and to value every aspect of life, even death.

It was Emma who had taught him patience, a virtue that was definitely needed with Tess, another woman he wanted in his life, a woman who was nearly as untouchable as Emma considering the barricades she put around herself.

He held the framed photograph of Emma to his chest and closed his eyes for a long moment as he allowed himself to relax. When he opened them, he saw Emma standing in the doorway. She wore the pretty purple nightgown he'd given her, and she silently stepped closer.

"Where have you been hiding?" he asked.

She merely offered him a soft smile. She drew closer and placed her hand on his chest, as if to tell him she was always in his heart. Her hand was warm, and she smelled of lilacs, as she so often did.

"I miss you," he said.

"I miss you, too," she whispered. "But I can't be with you now, and you need something more in your life besides work."

"But work keeps me busy. People die every day."

She sat down on the bed beside him. "But it doesn't get rid of your loneliness. I feel it, even here."

"It's not that bad."

She laughed, and the soft sound echoed off the silent walls. "You could never lie to me, M.D. So don't try now."

He smiled at the sound of the nickname she'd given him. M for Michael. D for Dwayne, his middle name after his father. Yet, she'd often teased that it was simply what he was meant to be—an M.D.

He reached out to touch her and thought he actually felt the softness of her curls. His fingertips brushed her cheek, and he felt that, too.

"She needs you."

"Who?" he asked.

"You need to ask?"

No, he didn't, he thought, but he said nothing.

Emma smiled, as if she read his thoughts. "Tess. And yes, I can talk about her with you. I can't be with you, but I don't want you to be alone. You're a wonderful man, and you deserve to be happy, so don't let the way she tries to shut out the world frighten you away. It's just what she's used to doing. She needs you. She just doesn't know how much, yet. She needs time to get close to you."

"How do you know?"

"Trust me."

"She's doesn't want me. I feel the way she hesitates when I invade her space or get too close. After she fainted, she would have rather fallen on her face than to be in my arms."

"I don't think that's true. Besides, she didn't move away when you kissed her. I think she wants to be in your arms. She's just afraid to be there."

"She has no reason to be afraid of me."

"So show her. Let her get to know you. It's not you. It's the closeness she fears, the closeness she can't trust."

"I don't want to scare her away." He brushed the softness of her cheek with the back of his fingers.

"Be patient."

"Maybe . . ."

Something banged three times on the front door and drew his attention and he jerked awake. The room was dark and he was alone.

Stiff and feeling groggy, haunted by the remnants of his dream of Emma, Michael sluggishly put his feet on the floor, only to step on Emma's picture. He let out a heavy breath and picked it up. Something compelled him to open the drawer of the nightstand and place the photo in there, face down. Then he forced himself to a standing position as more knocking reverberated through the house.

"All right, all right, I'm coming," he yelled as he shuffled out of his bedroom and toward the front door.

By the twilight darkness in the house, he realized he'd slept the entire day. Not only was the sun gone, but so was the clear, warm weather. He heard rain pelt against the roof, and the sound grew louder. When he opened the front door, cool, damp air rushed in.

As he stared outside, he saw rain coming down in what looked like solid sheets. But he barely noticed the rain because Tess stood on his front porch. Completely soaked from the downpour, her wavy hair and clothes were plastered to her.

And she stared at him with wide, fear-filled eyes that appeared too large for her face.

Chapter Three

Michael blinked at Tess several times, wondering if he was dreaming about her, just as he'd dreamed about Emma.

Then she opened her mouth as if to speak to him, but her teeth chattered instead. She was not only real, she was freezing.

He swore out loud and reached for her, deciding he didn't care whether or not she feared his invasion of her space. He grasped her arms and pulled her into house with him, gasping, "My God, Tess, you're freezing."

She wore a different tee shirt than she'd worn this morning, but her arms were still bare. Her skin was ice-cold and covered with goose bumps. Once he had her inside, she shivered uncontrollably.

"He keeps f-f-following me," she stammered.

His grasp still on one of her arms, he pulled her through his darkened house toward the bathroom. With the sudden flip of the switch, his bathroom filled with light that hurt his eyes, but he ignored it as he took in the woman before him.

She still shivered, and her teeth still chattered. Her face was as pale as the bodies on the slabs in his cooler, and her lips were slightly blue.

When he glanced down, he saw her nipples clearly through her wet shirt and did his best to ignore them. Then he let go of her just long enough to turn on the warm water to fill the tub. "Who's following you? When did you notice them? Did they follow you home from my house?" If his heart wasn't already pounding from finding her on his doorstep terrified and cold, it would have started pounding at the thought of someone stalking her.

"The m-m-man . . . the man f-f-f-from m-my vision."

Michael stopped short. If the idea of someone stalking her didn't scare him enough, this sent his heart into skids. "What? You've seen him? Did he follow you here? Is he still out there? Did you call Jake Williams? Never mind, I'll call him." He looked around, half expecting to find a man coming into the bathroom with them. What could he use for a weapon? The toilet plunger?

She shook her head. "It's not l-l-like that. I saw him when I tried to s-s-sleep. He was in my d-d-dreams, just like in the v-v-visions I have when I t-t-touch a dead p-p-person. But it went f-f-further than that. It continued when I was a-a-a-wake. Or at least when I t-t-thought I was a-a-awake and thought h-h-he was in my room. But t-t-then I went back to his h-h-house. I can't d-d-describe it. I don't e-e-even understand it. It's n-n-never happened like this b-b-before. It's l-l-like I'm connected to him s-s-somehow."

Michael bit his tongue before he swore again or started yelling at her for not calling him. Absently, he reached out and closed the bathroom door and locked it—just in case. "Let's take care of one thing at a time. Like getting you warm." It gave him something to do besides take her in his arms or shake her for not calling him or Jake. But this wasn't the time for recriminations. He needed to get Tess warm. "Get in the tub," he instructed.

She looked at the tub as if she'd never seen water before.

"You can leave your clothes on," he said. "Just take your shoes off."

She still didn't move.

He raked a hand through his hair. "Hell, Tess, I think you're in shock. I'll take you to the hospital and then call Jake."

"No!" she suddenly objected, but she didn't look away from the water. "I'll be all right."

"Yeah, right," he muttered. "Given the fact that you're paler than the victims I see everyday, I'd say you're right as rain," he said sarcastically. "I'm going to touch you, and I don't care if you don't like it. I don't care if it invades your personal space." What he really wanted to do was strip off both their clothes, climb into the tub and warm her with his body heat as well as the water. It would be the best and quickest way to keep her from suffering from hypothermia. But he knew he couldn't chance it. Right then she was too terrified, too vulnerable.

So with his hands on her shoulders, he moved her to sit

down on the closed commode. She didn't fight him. She didn't try to move away from him, either. One after another, he slipped off her running shoes and her socks, both of which dripped on the bathroom tile. "How did you get here?" Since he didn't dare pull her close, he did the next best think to keep her coherent. He forced her to talk to him.

"I drove."

"You got this wet and muddy driving over here? What did you do? Drive with the top down on your car?" He reached over and felt the temperature of the water in the tub. Perfect. He turned it off.

"I f-f-f-fell a few times."

At least her teeth weren't chattering as hard as they had been.

"Getting to my front door?" He helped her to stand, and she followed his lead without question. "Step in."

She did as he instructed as she said, "I f-f-fell once when I g-g-got out here."

"Sit down."

She did as he instructed and said, "It's h-h-hot."

"It's not that hot, and it will warm you up." The water sloshed and got his shirtsleeves wet.

"It b-b-burns my knees."

"Your knees?" She wore jeans, so he couldn't see her knees.

"I'm sure t-they're skinned."

Her words grew stronger, and he knew the water was warming her. In a few minutes, she'd be strong enough that he could leave her alone and go make her a hot cup of strong tea with sugar—lots of sugar.

"You skinned you knees when you fell getting to my front door? As soon as you're warm and you have on dry clothes, I'll take a look at them. I'm sure I have some antibiotic cream somewhere."

Her next words nearly stopped his heart, and they were twice as frightening because her teeth were no longer chattering.

"I fell twice at his house."

Michael touched her chin gently and turned her head so

she could meet his gaze. He had to force himself to breathe, as he asked hoarsely, "What did you say, Tess?"

"I fell at his house."

The flatness of her voice was just as frightening as her words. And if the warm water didn't help with the shock he felt filling her, he would take her to the hospital, whether she wanted to go or not.

"Did you really go to his house?" Michael could barely breathe. There was suddenly a vice squeezing his chest.

"Yes. I dreamed about it. I saw the number, and I saw the street. I saw his garage. It's big—big enough for him to park his van or truck or whatever he drives right inside, and he can drag or carry his victims into the house with no one seeing them."

Michael forced a painful breath past the lump in his throat. Then he forced out words as well, as he clinched his fists to keep from grabbing her arms and really shaking her this time. "Tess, what the hell were you thinking? You shouldn't have gone there. Don't you realize how dangerous that was? Next time, just take a dull knife and stick it in my chest, all right?"

He raked his fingers through his hair to give his hand something to do before he punched the damned wall. It took nearly every ounce of energy he had to keep his voice controlled and not scream at her for doing something so stupid, *so dangerous*.

Her eyes were incredibly large as she stared up at him, looking as if she might cry. "Don't talk about knives, okay?"

How stupid could he be? Michael wondered. The killer used a knife, and she'd not only seen what he did with it, when she'd touched the dead woman's hand, she'd felt it.

He again fought the urge to punch the wall, but this time it was because he was furious with himself. She was scared out of her wits, and she'd come to him for help. It was time he pulled himself together and acted like a professional instead of a jackass. "I'm sorry, Tess. What happened? Just tell me what happened."

"I had to find out if I'd really seen where he lived. I had to know that it wasn't all a dream, something my mind made up from lack of sleep or the fact that . . . you . . . you . . . kissed me. I've never had this happen before, and I couldn't send Jake Williams on some wild goose chase when I might be suffering from an overactive imagination."

"More reason to have called me or Jake—hell, anyone, even a neighbor—just to let someone know where you were and what you planned to do. God, Tess, don't do anything like that again! Please promise me you won't do anything like that again."

She stared at him with wide, fear-filled eyes. "You're really concerned for me." Her voice sounded so small, like a child who had just been sent to the principal's office and scolded.

"Yes, I'm concerned. You're damned right I'm concerned." He refused to fall prey to her soft voice. He couldn't. She had to realize she couldn't again put herself in that kind of danger.

Michael took a deep breath and forced calmness into his body and his voice before he let his fingers rest on the softness of her cheek. "What if he had seen you?"

"He didn't."

"How do you know that?"

"He didn't," she insisted.

Michael swallowed down his lingering anger. "I'm going to go call Jake. Are you all right if I leave you alone for a few minutes?"

"I'm fine."

She wasn't fine, but she had a little more color in her cheeks and her teeth weren't chattering any more. So he didn't think she would fall over and drown if he left her. "While I'm on the phone in the kitchen, I'll make you something warm to drink."

"No coffee."

"I wouldn't dream of it. Then I'll find you some clothes to wear." He didn't want to leave her. Truth be told, he wanted to take off his clothes, climb into the tub with her and remove her clothes. Then he could hold her against him, skin to skin, body to body, to make sure she warmed up all over. But that would probably send her flying out of the tub and out the front door and he'd never see her again. "I'll be right back."

He took his hand from her cheek, gave her hand a small

squeeze and moved away.

Hell, she looked so damned small and fragile in the water. He had no idea what was happening to her, but he decided right then and there that she wouldn't experience it alone. He'd go through this with her, even if he had to do it with her kicking and screaming—which was a real possibility.

In the kitchen, he put a cup of water into the microwave to heat and then dialed Jake's number. As the phone rang, he moved on to his bedroom where he managed to find some sweats that had a drawstring. Tess could cinch the waist and roll up the pants legs. He completed the ensemble with a pair of new white, thick tube socks.

He returned to the bath and found Tess standing in the tub, ready to climb out. As much as he would have liked to help her get out of her wet clothes, he simply set the sweats on the edge of the tub and pulled out a fresh towel. He also found the antibiotic cream in the medicine cabinet for her knees .

"Your tea should be ready by the time you've changed your clothes." He stepped out of the room, leaving the door open a few inches so he would hear her if she called for help.

Tess waited until Michael was gone before she reached up and grasped the edge of her tee shirt to pull it over her head. She'd only been out of the warm water mere moments, but her wet clothing was already cold. At least now, she felt the cold instead of feeling numb. Tess fought down a shiver and quickly stripped, dried off and put on the sweats and socks Michael had brought in. A few minutes later, with her hair towel dried, she stepped into Michael's warm kitchen. The subtle, lingering scent of the sausage they'd had for breakfast touched her like the heat of a crackling fire.

"Feel better?" he asked. He leaned casually against the counter, a mug in his hand.

"Yes, much. Thank you." She could tell by his clipped words, and the fact his knuckles were white as he gripped the mug, that he was still angry with her for her impulsive action despite his casual stance. That both irritated her and pleased her. She was used to being on her own, making her own decisions, but it was nice to have someone actually care about her safety.

"Here's your tea." He placed a second mug on the table and pulled out a chair for her. "Why don't you sit down? Jake will be here in a half hour or so."

Tess sat and reached out to grasp the cup of tea to warm her hands.

Michael, still holding his own cup, sat down across from her. "Care to tell me everything that happened or do you want to wait for Jake?"

Tess leaned forward, perched her elbow on the table and rested her chin on her hand. "So much of it runs together. I'm not sure where to start."

"Just start at the beginning."

Tess couldn't ignore the way he watched her closely, nor could she stop herself from eyeing him just as closely. He was unshaven, and she knew she'd awakened him with her arrival. He looked ruggedly handsome with his unruly hair and sharp features, and she suspected he missed nothing with his piercing blue eyes. She watched him as he absently combed his fingers through his hair, and she wondered what his hair would feel like if he allowed her to do the same. She swallowed down a hot, sweet gulp of tea and ignored the burning in her throat.

"I was antsy after I left here. I thought I was just overtired. But it was worse after I got home. I didn't understand, and I still don't. I thought I was just—"

"Just what?" he prodded when her voice trailed off.

She hesitantly met his gaze. Then she licked her lips. "I thought I was feeling that way because of your kiss. It's been a long time since I've been kissed. Touch for me is so . . . unique."

"I'm sure it is."

"Lips are exceptionally sensitive."

"I don't doubt it." He sounded almost as if the kiss they'd shared was no big deal, as if he was just agreeing with her to be polite.

Tess searched for the right words to get her point across. "I don't think you understand. Your kiss is still going through me, like an electrical current."

"It is?"

"Yes," she replied quickly. She had to lick her lips to bring some moisture to her mouth. And she still tasted him. "And I'm not telling you because it's a bad thing. I'm telling you because it's how I knew it was a safe thing."

He nodded. "Okay," he said slowly. "Go on. Explain how it's a safe thing."

She took a deep breath and let it out slowly, then afraid she might break the mug she held, she set it on the table. "First you need to understand that sometimes when I feel things, the feelings change as time goes on. It's like the layers of an onion. Then ten minutes later, I might feel something deeper, something different. Anyway, I thought the antsy feeling I had was from your kiss. And as time went on, that zingy, electrical, good feeling from the kiss never changed." Again she had to lick her lips. Her mouth was suddenly dry as a desert and her heart raced. She bit her lip absently and still the electrical current didn't fade. "It just got stronger," she let out in a whisper.

Then she cleared her throat and went on before he got the chance to interrupt. "Then my feelings did change, but the good feeling from the kiss didn't. Suddenly, my house seemed uncomfortable or empty. I wandered around inside for a while, then I went outside and walked around the yard. I felt as if I was being watched or something—something I can't define. I still can't put my finger on what I felt, and I can't find the words to describe it."

She paused and looked down to find that her hand was on the table, and his hand covered hers. She hadn't even known he'd moved, nor had she been aware of his sudden touch. How could he do that? How could he touch her and elicit no reaction when even an innocent brush in a crowded elevator sent her heart into overdrive?

Tess took a deep, even breath, and let his touch warm her. His warmth mingled with the electricity that still flowed through her. It reminded her of lying on a beautiful sunny beach with only the softness of sand, the sound of waves, and the blue sky above.

"I was more than antsy," she went on when he said nothing. She raised her gaze from their hands to his face. "I tried to read and couldn't. I turned on the television and turned it off after about a minute. I felt frustrated, as if I was looking for something I couldn't find. I laid down in my bed, then I got up. I took a shower, thinking that might relax me, but it didn't. I finally settled on the sofa. The next thing I knew, I jumped up off the sofa. I thought he—the killer from my vision—was in my house. Only it wasn't my house. It was my sofa in his house. The most horrible thing was, there weren't five women tied to chairs any more. There were four. Two chairs, the one I'd been in and the one where the redhead had sat next to me were both empty. None of the women could see me. I kept screaming at them, but I had no voice. I tried to untie them, but I couldn't. Something really strange happened then."

She stared at the window behind him, watched the downpour of rain. Suddenly, he squeezed her hand and softly asked, "What happened, Tess?"

Tess had to force in a breath, and she brought her attention back to his face. His expression was so concerned that it brought tears to her eyes. She blinked back the moisture and said, "It was as if he saw me, really saw me, there, even though that had never happened before. I moved through his house to avoid him, and he followed me. I tried to break the windows to get out, but I couldn't. They aren't glass but something else, something unbreakable. I continued to look for a way out, and he kept finding me. It was like this horrible game of hide-and-seek, and there was no place I could hide that he wouldn't find me. I hid in the closet in his bathroom. I expected to find towels and washcloths, toilet paper and things like that, but instead I found rolls of tape and wire and strange things like that."

Again her voice trailed off, and again he prodded her. "What happened then?"

"I'm not sure. Suddenly, I was back in the living room on my sofa, and he couldn't see me anymore. But I could see him, and I watched him drug the women, forcing them to swallow pills. When they were obviously out of it, I watched him unbind them and then tie them back up once they were free of the chairs. He dragged or carried or led them to a van in his garage. I stayed there until I heard his van leave. Then I walked out his front door. That's how I saw his house number and the street name."

She looked deeply into his eyes wanting nothing more than to get lost in the ocean she saw there, the ocean where she didn't have to face any of this horror. "I've never had a vision that followed me into my dreams. I jumped awake—I mean really awake this time—and I could have sworn he was in my house, as if he had followed me home. I looked in every room, and at the closet outside my bathroom—" Tess paused, remembering and shook her head as she ran her fingers through her hair in frustration. "I know this all sounds so crazy. It sounds crazy to me, and I'm the one who saw it."

"And nothing like this has ever happened before?" Michael asked.

"No, but I swear to you, this really happened. You have to believe me."

"It's not that I don't believe you. Just tell me what happened next. What about the closet?"

Tess let out another long breath. If Michael didn't believe her, she didn't know what she'd do. She had nowhere else to go, no one else to trust. Jake might believe her, would even follow up on any lead she gave him, but it was Michael's safety and warmth she now craved. "I stood there for several minutes with my hand on the knob." She had to pause to force down a swallow. "The door was open a few inches, like his had been. Only this door is never open. It's a really close hallway and the door being open makes it almost impossible to get through. I was so certain that when I opened the door I would find him— or that I would at least find his rolls of tape and wire. But when I finally found the courage to pull it open, it was just my linen closet."

She reluctantly slid her hand from beneath his, lifted her cup with both hands and took another sip of tea to warm her insides. She felt as if her teeth would start chattering again.

"But you still thought he was in your house?" Michael asked.

He sounded merely curious, and, thankfully, not as if he didn't believe her.

Tess nodded and sighed. "Yes. I felt him in every room, all around me."

"Damn, that must have felt spooky as hell," he muttered.

Tess set her mug back on the table, and when she put her hand down on the table again, Michael reached out without hesitation and took her hand in his. With his touch, she felt a storm of emotions—worry, concern, exasperation, and above all else, fear. But this time he didn't reprimand her. "Spooky? It scared me to death. I couldn't stay there."

"So let me guess what happened next. This guy has terrified you, and instead of calling me or Jake, or just coming over here like you finally did, you went looking for his house. It wasn't enough that he scared you to death, you wanted to give him the opportunity to catch you, right?"

She ignored his sarcasm, sensing his underlying fear and knowing instinctively it was fear for her safety.

"Not exactly," she replied. "I couldn't get the image of being in his house, of watching him drug those women, out of my head. I slipped on my shoes and picked up my keys and ran outside. It was afternoon, and it was starting to rain. At first, I just drove aimlessly. Then it was like I picked up his feelings— or his essence—again. And suddenly there I was on South Lindell Street, standing out in the rain in front of his house, with the house number in gold stickers on his mailbox."

He squeezed her hand. She again marveled at his touch. It felt like a lifeline. She shifted her hand so she could hold his tighter. His heat, his strength, grounded and warmed her. He said nothing, seeming to know she needed his touch, not his words.

Finally, she continued her story. "I have no idea how long I stood there in front of his house—which definitely is in need of painting—while the world just grew darker and darker, and the rain came down harder and harder. Then I thought I had to know for sure. I had to see."

"Oh, damn." His words were little more than a breath. He covered his eyes with his free hand while he squeezed her hand again. "Tell me you didn't go up to the house."

"I did. I walked around. I looked in the windows." Tess

paused and shivered violently.

"Take a drink," Michael instructed. He finally looked at her, hard. "If I didn't have to let go of you, I'd get us something stronger than tea with sugar. I know I definitely need something stronger."

Tess clung to his hand while she took a drink of her tea and let its warmth seep to her middle. But it couldn't stop the chill that passed over her at the memory of the killer's house. "When I looked through the windows, I saw the chairs where all the women were tied. I saw his living room. I saw into his bathroom and saw the closet where I hid from him in the dream. The only thing missing was my sofa."

"And did you see him?"

Tess heard fear in Michael's voice, and she had to clear her throat before she could go on because she shared it. "No. He's gone. He's taken them somewhere else." She met Michael's gaze. "I think he felt me, Michael. He somehow knew I was there. I think that's why he left." She again shivered violently.

Michael reluctantly let go of her hand, stood and walked out of the kitchen. A moment later, he returned with a cotton throw, obviously from the living room. Gently, he wrapped the warm cover about her shoulders. His hands lingered on her arms as he settled it around her, the heat of them reaching her through the layer of cotton.

"Better?" he asked.

"Much, thank you." This time it was her turn to reach out and take his hand while he stood gazing down at her. "I know what you're thinking."

"Now you can read my mind?"

"It's not hard to do. You're very easy read, so you should never play poker," she teased. Then she sobered and said, "You're thinking I was stupid for not calling Jake Williams as soon as I saw the killer's house in my dream."

"Not stupid," he corrected. "Foolish, maybe, and definitely careless. I think you should have called Jake or me, or better yet, 9-1-1, as soon as you woke up and felt that the killer was in your house. Hell, if you thought *anyone* was in your house, you should have just gotten out of there. And you certainly shouldn't have searched the house looking for him. What would you have done if you had found him hiding in your closet?"

"I don't know. I guess I would have run then."

Michael moved around the table and again sat down across from her. He didn't hesitate to reach out to her and they held hands again. "It might have been too late for that." He paused. "Tess, this man is dangerous. What if he'd really been in your house? Or what if he'd still been at his house? What if he'd seen you or grabbed you? When I think that right now you could be tied to one of the chairs or worse . . . well, that scares the hell out of me. And if he had captured you, we wouldn't have even known where to start looking for you."

Filled with guilt, she looked down at her cup of tea. "I know. But the entire experience was so bizarre. Like I said before, I couldn't seem to get a grip on what was real and what wasn't. I needed to be sure about what I'd seen before I talked to anyone about it."

He reached out and, with two fingers, gently lifted her chin, forcing him to look at him. "Yes, well, I'd hate for you to be dead sure. And you don't have to do any of this alone. I've seen your ability. I've seen how you work. Please don't shut me out. Let me help you determine what's real and what isn't." His voice was calm and his words even, although they were still laced with a subtle hint of fear and concern.

"All right," she agreed. "Especially since I'm not even sure what happened or how. I just know it was so terrifying to think perhaps he could see me somehow. And I don't even know if I can do it again. But if he could really see me, I think that sooner or later, he'll simply know where I am."

"Now that's making me feel warm all over," he muttered, but he refused to let her see how cold and terrified the idea left him.

"I just wish I knew how to do it again."

"What?" Michael thought that until she did learn to control whatever new ability this was, he might have to act like the killer and tie her to a chair in order to keep her safe.

"Well, if I could do it again, and I could control it, I could keep him from finding me or getting too close. Yet, I could lure him to where the police could catch him."

"I certainly hope you're right about keeping him from finding you. In the meantime, I hope Jake stops him before we have to worry about him getting close."

She nearly jumped out of her chair as the peal of the doorbell rang through the house.

Chapter Four

"It's okay. I'm sure it's just Jake." Michael let go of Tess's hand to go answer the door. A moment later, Jake followed Michael into the kitchen.

"You look awful," Tess stated with forced casualness.

"Thanks," Jake replied. "You look like Sally Sunshine, too."

Jake had dark hair that curled at his collar. Tess often thought he was a good-looking man with eyes darker than his hair and bronze skin, except for the fact that police work somehow gave him a beaten, worn-down appearance. She recalled he'd once mentioned having a wife. How could love survive the day in and day out, twenty-four hour on call exposure to murder and violence? Did Jake manage to leave his work at the office where it belonged? She certainly hoped so.

"Want something to drink?" Michael offered.

"I'd love a beer or even something stronger like a double Scotch on the rocks. But I'd better hold off until I get home. Do you have a soda?"

"Dark or light?"

"Whatever has the most caffeine."

A moment later, Michael handed Jake a cola. Tess and Michael continued to drink tea. Michael refilled Tess's cup and added more sugar. For a long moment, none of them said anything. They merely drank their drinks and reflected in the silence that was broken only by the soft sounds of the muffled rain.

"So what happened?" Jake asked.

Tess told him all she could remember about feeling out of place in her house, then dreaming of the killer and his hostages, before moving on to the part where she awoke and felt his presence in her own home. She gave his address and confessed to going there and looking around.

When Jake glared at her, his pursed lips and narrowed brow told her he thought what she'd done was a stupid, dangerous move, but he didn't say the words. Instead, he wrote the address in his notebook before he pulled out his cell phone and relayed the information to his team.

Then he looked squarely at Tess. "Markus Black from the FBI, is now working on this with me since we've been able to tie this killer to several other unsolved murders. He'll head to that address as soon as he can get his hands on a warrant. Is there anything else you can tell me about this man? Where he might have taken his hostages, what he's driving?"

Tess shook her head. "His garage was dark. I think I saw a van, but I can't be sure. Whatever it was, it was dark, too, black or dark blue or maybe even dark gray or green. I'm really not sure."

"Has anything like this ever happened to you before? This idea that you're connected to the killer, and not through a dead person?" Jake asked before he took a long swallow of soda.

"No."

"Did you get a better look at the killer so you can upgrade the sketch that was drawn this morning?"

"Not really. He's nervous, antsy. He never looks directly at his victims, and they don't look at him. And his hair is long—it hangs in his face. Not to mention, I was busy trying to avoid him."

Michael spoke for the first time. "Tess, is there a possibility you somehow connected to another victim, one who's not dead yet or possibly the missing redhead, and not to the killer?"

Jake swallowed hard enough for Tess to see his Adam's apple move as he shifted his gaze to Michael. "I wonder that, too, because we found a body matching the description of one of the women you said you saw tied to a chair."

For a long moment, Tess thought she might throw up the tea she'd just swallowed. "You're talking about the woman who was missing when I had my dream, aren't you?"

* * * *

"Are you sure you're up to going back to the morgue?" Michael asked a short time later. He still held her hand. It seemed like a small action, and yet if it gave her a sense of safety, it was worth the effort. Besides, he loved the feel of her.

"I don't have much of a choice," Tess replied.

She sounded stronger to him, but he hated that she felt obligated to do this. "You have every choice," Michael argued as he drove. "It hasn't even been twenty-four hours since we were there."

"I know—since I was there taking the hand of murder victim. And honestly, no, I'm not ready to take another hand," Tess replied.

He glanced at her only to find her looking over at him, and she said, "But if it will help Jake stop him, then I can do it. As long as you're there with me."

"I'll be there to catch you if you faint, don't worry," he responded, offering her a small smile in an effort to lighten the mood.

"Do you really think it was necessary for me to put my car in your garage?" she asked.

Michael glanced into the rearview mirror and noticed he'd lost Jake a few blocks back. He didn't wait to make the next turn. Jake knew his way to the morgue. "If this guy can somehow see you and sense you or even find you at your house, maybe he can find you anywhere, but we don't need to make it easy for him."

They reached the parking lot and Michael parked as close to the door as possible before killing the engine.

"The morgue looks creepy at night with the rain," Tess observed.

Michael noticed she stared at the building and didn't move to open her door. He climbed out and opened it for her just as a distant roll of thunder rumbled through the night. "I won't leave you alone, Tess," he promised. He reached out a hand to her.

Slowly, Tess placed her hand his. She could do this with him beside her. And yet, he rolling thunder still sounded like a monster trying to get in, Tess thought, as they hurried toward the building. As they moved together down the hall, Tess was almost positive the killer would suddenly leap out in front of them. The thought caused the hair on the back of her neck to stand on end.

The morgue was well lit, but the light didn't seem to shake off the murk. Dr. Riley Turner was now on duty. Dr. Turner was probably fifty, but she looked more like thirty-five to forty, with her trim, lean build and nearly wrinkle-free face. Her gray-white hair was covered with a cloth medical cap and small wisps had escaped around her ears. One of her death investigators, Ellen—Tess didn't know Ellen's last name—was in Dr. Turner's office with her. Tess and Michael greeted them as they moved past.

"Get bored on your vacation already, Michael?" Riley asked.

Michael grinned. "On Detective Jake Williams's authority, we're just here to take a look at the latest victim."

"He thinks this is the work of a serial killer, doesn't he?"

"It looks as if it may be. And he thought that since I examined the last victim, it might be helpful if I take a look at this one, too. He should be here any minute."

"That's fine. Ellen and I were just taking a break. There was a triple homicide, and we spent the last two hours at the crime scene in the rain. And the mortuary showed up earlier claiming those kids, so the cooler's emptying out and . . ."

Riley had a way of talking so much and so fast in a voice so high she ground on everyone's nerves, so Tess blocked out the rest of what Riley spent the next several minutes saying. She also blocked out whatever Michael politely answered. She couldn't deny it any longer—she couldn't fight off the need to touch Michael. It was as if he called out for her touch. She squeezed his hand. He squeezed back.

The action sent a river of warmth right up her arm and into her body. When he leaned closer, brushing the entire length of his arm against hers, he very well could have touched her soul. She let him lead her away from Riley's office and down the hall to the stairs that led to the cooler.

"You're awfully quiet," he noted. "Are you all right?"

"My shoes are still wet, and I'm cold again," she admitted. "When this is over, I think I'll take a vacation in the desert."

He paused, turned and met her gaze. The compassion Tess saw in his eyes and his expression touched her as deeply as the strength she felt in his hand as he held hers.

"When we get done with this, I'll take you back home and make you some soup," he told her. Then he glanced down at her soaked feet. "And we'll get you a dry pair of shoes on the way."

"That sounds wonderful," Tess lied. Right then, anything she ate probably wouldn't stay down. But the thought of just being in his home with him warmed her. Being anywhere with Michael, besides here in the hall leading to the cooler, would be great, she thought. Why did the bricks of the wall have to be a cool blue color? Why did the lights have to be dim? She fought down a shiver as she tried not to look at them as they moved to the swinging doors.

To Tess, the cooler never changed—bright lights reflected off the silver metal slabs and counters, the off-white walls, and the large silver refrigerator doors that took up the entire far wall. And the glare hurt her eyes after the hall's dank lighting. Michael still held her hand while he glanced at the clipboard inside the door before he led her to a nearby slab. Tess did her best to breathe shallowly and lessen the pungent smell of formaldehyde.

As she stared down at the draped body on the slab, she suddenly felt a rush of fear that nearly buckled her knees. "Michael?"

"Yes?"

"You won't leave me?"

"Not on your life."

She slowly met his gaze. "If I faint again, please don't let anyone upstairs see me."

"I won't. I promise. Do you want to see her face?"

Tess took a heavy breath. It calmed her nerves, but the room's pungent odor burned her nose. "Yes."

Before he could pull back the sheet, Jake slipped through the door and into the room. "Did I miss anything?" he whispered.

"No, you didn't, and you don't have to whisper in here, Jake," Michael pointed out.

Jake looked around. "Yes I do."

With his free hand, Michael pulled back the sheet that covered the victim, revealing the redhead from Tess's dream. "The girl in the chair next to me," Tess said.

"You're sure?" Jake sounded startled.

"Yes." She licked her lips but failed to bring any moisture to her mouth. And when she tried to swallow, she found it impossible. Then she reached out.

But Michael caught her hand, drawing her gaze to him as he said, "You know, you don't have to do this."

She smiled sadly. "I have to do it. If I don't, it will be like only putting together half a puzzle."

Before he could say more, she slipped her hand from his and reached out and took the woman's cold one . . .

* * * *

The dirty aquarium came into view. There were four gold fish swimming in it. She stared at them and tried to control her breathing. She also tried to control the burn of the bile that rose in her throat. Her heart pounded painfully and dark spots danced before her eyes.

He'd just killed Jill. Just like that.

She looked down at her own legs. Her bare flesh was covered with goose bumps.

And splattered with drops of Jill's blood.

She was unable to stop the groan that moved through her vocal cords.

"Julie, shut up," the girl next to her said in a rough, terror-filled whisper.

Tess, now Julie, didn't have to groan. The sounds of her own raspy breathing filled the room. Any moment, she thought she might be sick, despite the fact that she'd not eaten in more than a day. Slowly, she turned to her left and took in the girl next to her. She had short, blond spiked hair and fierce brown eyes.

"He just killed her, Anna." Julie forced out, trying to keep her voice low and finding she had very little control left. Her throat was simply too tight. The terror was cold, like claws that dug through her. She tried not to cry, but couldn't stop the tears that slid down her cheeks.

"Yeah, like we all didn't just see him do it. Now shut up before he comes back and hears you. We can't help her anymore, but we've got to do what we can to help each other." Anna's voice was a little louder, but still working to remain soft.

"I can't. I can't." She couldn't breathe, either. Nor could she stop shivering. The next thing she heard was screaming. It took several moments to realize the screams came from her. They were piercing and shrill for several moments before they turned into words. "Help! Someone help us! Help! Help us!"

Her chair was grasped from behind. The action startled her, and she screamed louder. He leaned right over her, his face mere inches from hers, his greasy, long hair hanging in his face. His breath was acidic, and she gasped at the sour smell that told her he needed a shower and to brush his teeth.

"We're going to play a new game before we all go on a hike," he said. "I know how much all of you love to hike. It will be a wonderful trip down memory lane."

His knife loomed into her vision, and she screamed again. He brought it down, but she felt no pain. She saw, to her amazement, he used it to cut the plastic that bound her wrists to the chair. "The game's called hide-and-seek. I'm sure I don't have to tell you how to play. I'll give you to the count of ten." He was quiet for a long moment.

In the silence, she thought she could hear her heart pounding.

"One. Two."

She shot out of the chair and raced to the door. Her legs were weak from lack of use, as well as lack of food and water; and she nearly stumbled. She leaned against the door to stay horizontal.

"Three."

The door was locked with a deadbolt that required a key to unlock it.

"Four."

There was a small table beside the sofa in the living room, and she grasped it and slung it with all her strength at the living room window. It merely bounced away, not even making a crack in the glass.

"It's Plexiglas," the man announced. "Five. Six."

She raced through to the kitchen and opened drawers looking for a weapon, anything to use against him. Every drawer was empty.

"Seven, eight, lay them straight." His voice happily rang through the house and sent more shivers up her spine. He clearly enjoyed this. The house was strangely empty and his words and laughter echoed around her.

She ran to the bathroom. There was no lock on the door. The window was nailed shut and the pane was Plexiglas, too.

"Nine, ten. Here I come again."

She pulled open the bathroom closet door. Expecting to find towels or toilet paper or bars of soap, she was taken back by the black tape and bundles of plastic fasteners. Without wasting more time, she stepped into the closet and hid, her own rapid breathing filling the dark silence.

When he pulled open the door a moment later and yelled, "Olly, olly, oxen free," she barreled into him with all her strength. She scratched and kicked and fought.

But it was just like trying to bash in the Plexiglas. In the end, she lost . . .

* * * *

Tess opened her eyes and sucked in a loud, heavy gasp. Her hand felt glued to the dead woman's, and she had to pry it away.

"Tess?"

"Ooooohhh . . ." She fell into Michael's arms. She clung to his shirt and pressed her face to his chest as she relished in the sound of his strong, steady heartbeat, the soft scent of fabric softener and the clean man smell she recognized as Michael. His blue aura, his warmth, and his scent touched her like the soothing water of a whirlpool.

"Take a few easy breaths." Beneath her cheek, his chest vibrated with his words.

At first his voice sounded far away, but it grew closer with each breath she took. "I didn't faint this time."

"No, but another few seconds of not breathing, and you

probably would have."

Tess closed her eyes and still allowed him to hold her. "My dream wasn't a vision, exactly. It was more like I was dreaming it as it was happening to her. He forced her to play hide-and-seek. He found her in the bathroom closet."

From across the room came Jake's voice. "I hope you got a better look at him this time."

"I did, kind of, and a few other things, too." Tess still didn't let go of Michael. She hoped she never had to let go of Michael. Despite his warmth, she shivered uncontrollably.

* * * *

She was still shivering an hour later. Michael sat with her at police headquarters. The place was busy and loud and bustling, as usual—at least outside the double doors Jake had ushered them through. Tess drank hot chocolate made with hot water and mix, and it tasted like cardboard and barely reached, much less warmed, her middle. She kicked off her wet shoes and flexed her sock-covered toes against the floor. She hadn't taken off her coat. And she had never let go of Michael's hand.

"You're sure these women know each other?" Jake asked her, gesturing toward boards at the front of the room.

Their pictures were posted on the boards—the deceased victims on one side and the missing victims on the other. The women had been identified by matching missing persons' reports with Tess's information. On the middle board was a more detailed drawing of the suspect, also thanks to Tess's information.

"Yes, they know each other," she confirmed.

"And you think it's more than just the fact that he introduces them when he brings them together?"

"Yes."

"How can you be sure?"

At the sound of the voice from behind her, Tess's heart raced nearly as fast as it had in her vision. She would know that voice anywhere. It still haunted her dreams and she had hoped to never hear it again. She swallowed down the panic that threatened her and forced herself to remain still. She wouldn't even give him the satisfaction of turning and facing him. She wasn't even aware she was squeezing Michael's fingers until he attempted to turn and see the speaker, but her grip allowed him to move very little. She forced in a heavy breath and licked her lips as Markus Black strode to the front of the room.

To Tess, the man had changed very little. His hair, although cropped shorter than she remembered, was still sandy. His skin was tanned, as if he'd just strolled in off the beach, and the gold of his skin was heightened by the dark, perfect suit he wore. His confidence was like a billboard that stated: God's gift to mankind is here.

"Hello, Tess," he addressed her.

"Markus," she let out, doing her best to keep the single word from sounding clipped. She would never let him or anyone else know how much he rattled her. It had been four years since she'd walked out on him. Inwardly, she smiled as she discovered it wasn't her time with him that still bothered her. What bothered her—what rattled her most—was the idea of how he probably hadn't changed much, that he still used women at every opportunity.

Markus looked at Michael as if he'd suddenly noticed Michael beside her. "I'm FBI Special Agent Markus Black."

"Michael Adams."

Markus turned his attention back to Tess. "Please don't be offended when I tell you that we have put every possible bit of information on these women into the computer. There is nothing linking them together. There is nothing that even indicates they could be acquainted, much less know one another on a personal basis."

"And I'm telling you they do."

"Because you saw it in a vision, right?" He asked the question slowly, as though interrogating her.

The question grated on Tess's last nerve. "At times, yes. You know I do."

"And that makes you a psychic?"

"I don't put a label on it, Agent Black. I simply help out the homicide detectives when I can." Her throat was suddenly tight. She thought she might choke. She forced her hand to release the paper cup of hot chocolate before she squeezed the edges together and spilled it on the table.

"Agent Black? Tess told us about a vision where it appears that the last two victims and the hostages know one another's names." Jake put in.

"That doesn't mean they've known each other more than the few days he's held them hostage."

Tess squeezed Michael's hand and drew in a slow breath. She was immediately calmed by the way Michael squeezed her hand back. "What you say is true, Agent Black. The killer could have introduced them. He could have even served them tea and had a little party. But I heard the way they talked to one another. I heard the way they addressed one another. They didn't stumble over names. They didn't hold back from telling each other what to do. I'm telling you, the feeling I got from what I saw is that these women have known each other for a long time. And he's known them. He talked about taking them all on a hike because, quote-unquote, they all like to hike. That wasn't random."

Markus Black looked at her as if she was sprouting purple horns out the top of her head.

Jake cleared his throat as he moved to the board filled with photographs. "From all indications, Julie Olson grew up in Florida. She was abducted from a grocery store parking lot outside of Tallahassee a week ago. And Anna Carpelli grew up here in Illinois. She was reported missing by her husband when her boss called looking for her because she failed to show up at the law firm where she worked. That was three days ago. Her briefcase was found next to her car in the parking lot outside the law firm. But if Tess thinks these women somehow know each other, then I think they do."

"Thank you, Jake," Tess murmured gratefully.

Markus shook his head. "Olivia Brannigan lives in Indiana. Shanna Brown lives in Missouri. Sue Harper, the first one to be reported missing, lived here in Chicago. And the previous victim, Jill St. James lived in southern Illinois, nowhere near Anna Carpelli. There is nothing these women have in common.

They never went to the same school. They don't even attend the same church. Give me one example where they can be acquainted."

"Perhaps they all belong to the same chat room," Jake suggested.

"My team is checking their computers as we speak, at least the ones that haven't been checked yet," Agent Black said. "But that's pretty unlikely, too, since according to her husband, Shanna Brown doesn't even use a computer. She and her husband own a bakery and she decorates cakes. He does the bookkeeping."

"Maybe they all belong to a hiking group," Tess offered. "When the man said he and the other women were going on a hiking trip, he sounded sarcastic, but perhaps they all really do like to hike." Tess knew that sounded just as farfetched as everything else, but right then she was grabbing at straws. What she really wanted to do was figure out a way to get Markus Black to listen to her. Her insides felt raw and her head ached, but she wanted to find a way to catch the killer before he killed again. The last thing she wanted was to have to grasp another one of his victims' hands.

"We're checking on that, too." Jake said, still standing near the board as if there were answers in the photographs. " Tess, is s there anything else you can remember, anything at all, that can lead us in some direction to find this guy?"

Tess shook her head. "Not right now. Maybe it will be like before, and as time goes on, I'll remember more. But for now, I've told you everything I can recall. What about his house?"

"We should have the warrant within the hour, but that's no concern of yours," Agent Black replied.

Tess swallowed down a burning taste of bile. *No concern?* She wanted to scream. She'd been in that house, at least psychically. She'd seen the fish in the aquarium, and she would never forget the house's locker room smell or the dusty, dirty feel of it. It would haunt her dreams, and Agent Black had the gall to tell her it was no concern of hers.

She was about to tell him he could take his opinions and go to hell, but Michael shifted and brushed his arm against hers as he said, "Tess, I don't want you anywhere near that bastard's house. I'm worried about your safety." He let go of her hand just enough to lace his fingers through hers.

Tess closed her eyes briefly and allowed his tenderness and vitality, his goodness, and his true concern, surge through her as his heat moved through her.

"So am I," Jake said, as he turned away from the board and looked at her. "That's why I'm putting you under police protection."

"I'm not staying here." Tess gripped Michael's hand as she would grip a life ring in the middle of raging ocean waves. "And I'm not staying in some hole-in-the-wall safe house or cheap hotel room, either."

"You can stay with me." There was no hesitation in Michael's voice.

She met his gaze and couldn't help smiling despite the seriousness of the situation.

"That would work," Jake said. "And I'll assign a patrol to guard you."

"Do you really think all that is necessary?" Tess asked.

Jake shrugged. "I'd rather not find out the hard way that it is."

Tess nodded and concentrated on the distinct sensation of Michael's hand. His skin was warm and leathery soft. In his fingers, she felt his energy. Like the heat and light of a bonfire, it drew her to him and sent small bursts of something like an electrical current into her hand and up her arm. Those currents were strong enough to cause her heart to skip a beat. She hated to let go, but she had no choice. She needed both hands to put on her wet shoes.

"Are you leaving, Tess?" Jake asked.

"Yes."

"We aren't finished," Markus Black put in.

Tess met his gaze evenly and defiantly. "I'm wet, I'm cold and I'm hungry. And I think that no matter how long I stay here, I'm not going to convince you these women know one another. So I'm finished." Tess tied her shoe. "Michael?"

"Yes?"

"Take me home, please."

His warm hand was suddenly on the small of her back as
he ushered her toward the door. The warmth of his touch slid
easily to the middle of her belly and suddenly made breathing
hard.

"Tess?" Markus Black attempted to stop her.

She held up a hand, surprised her action stopped him from
saying more. "Jake, you have my cell number, and I'm sure
you have Michael's. Call me if you need anything urgent. Good
night, gentlemen."

Michael's maintained his hold on her hand all the way to
his car where Tess finally allowed herself to relax. Neither
said a word. It was as if all they needed was to touch hands in
order to remain connected, no conversation was needed.

Michael took her home.

To his home.

* * * *

Tess loved Michael's bathroom, with its dark wood trim. It
smelled like orange furniture polish, Michael's aftershave, soap
and the subtle scent that was Michael—soft, outdoorsy and
enticing. The shower was huge, a walk-in room with gray walls
and a small bench. The spray covered her completely coming
from three bars that surrounded her and looked like small pipes
with holes in them. The water was wonderful. Hot and steamy,
it worked its warmth into her soul. Every now and then, a
rumble of thunder from the storm outside managed to penetrate
the even rush of the water spray. Tess finally stepped out into
the steamy bathroom and wrapped herself in a plush towel.
The rug beneath her feet was soft. She noticed the big tub
across the room. She'd been so terrified and cold when Michael
put her in the tub earlier in the day that she hadn't even noticed
the shower or the deep, rich yellow of the walls. Gosh, his
bathroom was nearly as big as her kitchen.

A loud, close crack of thunder startled her just before the
lights went out. The darkness swallowed her instantly. Tess let
out a startled cry. She stood still gripping the towel tightly. She
was startled a second time when Michael tapped on the door.
Her gasp was enough to bring him in holding a glowing candle

in one hand while he had clothes tucked up under his arm.

"It's okay," he told her as he held the clothes out to her. "The power's just out from the storm. I found more clean sweats for you, and I put your wet shoes in the dryer. They were thumping away in there until the lights went out. I'll take them out and set them in the laundry room so they can dry on their own."

"Thank you."

Michael peered at her through the darkness, his eyes reflecting the glow of the candle he held. He appeared just a bit menacing in dark jeans and a black sweater. And yet, at the same time, she was drawn to him as she'd never before been drawn to anyone. In fact, with her history of shying away from people, the desire—the very need—to step closer to him left her slightly dizzy with confusion.

He studied her, and Tess could only imagine what she must look like—a drowned rat?

"In the second drawer below the sink, you'll find a new toothbrush and the toothpaste."

"Were you expecting an overnight guest?" Tess asked, realizing she knew nothing about his personal life. Suddenly, she wanted to know. She also wanted to move closer, rest her head on his chest and listen to the steady beat of his heart.

"No, I just happened to get lucky with a two for one sale." He studied her for another moment. Then, before she could step closer and feel the softness of his sweater against her cheek, he set the candle on the nearby counter and left the room with a gruff, "Let me know if you need anything else."

Tess took a deep breath, not knowing until then that she'd even been holding it. She looked into the mirror at her reflection, lit only by a single candle. She didn't like the dark. She liked it even less when she was forced into it.

Could the killer find her in the dark? She ignored the disturbing question and dressed quickly.

A short time later, she stepped out of the bath and through Michael's bedroom, led into the kitchen by the enticing aroma of chicken noodle soup. Her stomach grumbled. Three candles on the table, two more on the counter and one near the stove lit the kitchen and cast a warm, inviting glow that sent flickering shadows across the walls.

"How'd you heat the soup?" she asked.

Michael turned from where he stood at the counter and poured soup from a pan into two bowls. "The stove's gas."

"Oh. It smells wonderful." She looked out his back door. Darkness had settled over the neighborhood like a cold mantle, and rain still showered against the roof. Lightning lit up the sky, and thunder rumbled in reply as the storm grew in intensity and threatened to swallow the city. A few small sticks, an empty bag, and several leaves blew across the backyard.

Tess stood looking out his window and worked to calm her nerves. The energy of the growing storm merely added to her tension and left her feeling frazzled. The charge felt so strong, she thought that if her hair wasn't still wet, it might stand on end.

Michael came up behind her and grasped her arms. "Are you all right?"

"Yes—no," she admitted. "I feel cold, but hot. I feel antsy as hell, like I did at my house earlier. At the same time, I'm tired. I keep telling myself I'm safe, that there's no way the killer could ever know I'm here, and even if he did, there are cops parked right out front. Then I feel like there're bugs crawling all over me, and all of a sudden I think that he's going to come walking down your hallway and I start to panic."

Michael put his arms around her gently, and Tess let him. In fact, she nearly fell into his embrace. Like a moth drawn to flame, she was simply drawn to his heat and the steady beat of his heart. Why should he feel so good? Why should she need or even want to be close to him?

Tess didn't have to wonder at that question. He was good, and with her world suddenly nothing but chaos, she was drawn to his goodness like a cat drawn to a warm spot of sunshine.

"He can't get in," he assured her. "He can't get past the cops out front. Come eat your soup. You'll feel better."

After several bites, Tess did feel better.

Across the table from her, in the soft glow of the candles, Michael grinned. "It's not exactly the picnic we planned, is it?"

Tess couldn't help chuckling. "No." She met his gaze over the small flames. To Tess, the candles represented more positive energy. In fact, everything around Michael seemed to overflow with positive energy. "But it's nice."

And while eating her soup in his warm kitchen with his positive energy surrounding her, she didn't feel the dirty bugs of the killer crawling on her skin.

* * * *

After they ate, they moved to Michael's living room. Tess stood at his front window and looked out at the dark street. The police cruiser was hardly more than a silhouette lost in the shadows. After Michael lit candles on the fireplace mantle, he drew her close again and held her to him. As Tess leaned against him, she concentrated on the sound of his heart beating. It sounded as strong and sure as the man. She might have spent a life of being shunned, of never being able to trust, but accepting Michael and being close to him was easy.

"Come sit down."

She let him lead her to the couch and she sat with him, relishing in his closeness.

"I checked all the doors and windows. Everything's locked up," he said. "So don't worry."

"Easy for you to say."

He pressed up against the entire length of her side, and Tess felt as if she could melt into him. Everything about him was growing more familiar with each touch.

"We could play cards or something." Michael said softly. Then he chuckled. "That sounded pretty lame, didn't it?"

"Only a little." She smiled at him.

"Are you warm enough?"

"Yes, the soup did the trick. Thanks."

"You look tired."

She gave him a small smile. "I feel like I ran a marathon all day." She didn't point out that she really felt as if the killer had chased her the distance of a marathon.

Michael was so close she felt the warmth of his breath on her neck, just below her ear. She felt a tingle move up her back. A moment later, she felt the gentle touch of his fingers as he absently brushed her hair away from her face.

Before she could draw in a breath, he tilted her chin up and touched his lips to hers. His kiss sent her heart pounding and her chest grew tight. For a long moment, he simply pressed his lips to hers, unmoving, as if he knew she needed time to adjust and grow accustomed to the wild surge of energy that suddenly rolled through her like a great ball of fire.

Need filled her. Longing, like she'd never known before, touched her and brought goose bumps to her arms and legs. She nearly shivered. At the same time, she was suddenly so hot she thought might burst into flame.

He held her closer to him, deepened his kiss. The tickle of his tongue against hers sent another shiver through her. It was as if she were an instrument, and he knew how to play it— very well.

With all the strength Tess could gather, she forced herself away from him. He still held her in his arms. Her breathing sounded loud in the room, nearly as loud as the beating rain drumming a rhythm on the roof. She worked to bring her breathing under control.

"I'm sorry." Michael's words sounded breathy, too.

She shook her head, unable to speak for a moment. She was unable to meet his gaze, not wanting him to see her vulnerability. "Don't be. It's just me. You don't understand what your touch does to me."

"Why don't you explain it to me, then? And you can start by explaining Markus Black."

Tess met his gaze in a snap and stared at him for a long moment. As casually as possible, she asked, "What makes you think there's anything to explain about Markus Black?"

Michael wondered if he should let the subject drop as she looked at him through wary eyes, but he sensed this was something important, something he needed to pursue. "I saw the way you reacted to him when he came into the room at police headquarters. More importantly, I was holding your hand, and I *felt* the way you reacted."

She looked away, and he cupped her cheek gently in the palm of his hand. "No, don't turn away from me. Don't you know your actions speak so much louder than any words could have?"

It tore at his gut that he couldn't get through to her. It tore at him more to know he might be scaring her away. His lips still sizzled from her kiss. His entire body felt alive as if he'd just been plugged into a wall socket and two hundred and twenty volts now rushed through him. He wanted her, pure, simple and primitively—very primitively. He could make a fire in the fireplace, and the two them could lay before it while he undressed her—slowly. While he kissed every inch of her and tasted all there was to taste. While he touched and explored until the two of them were skin to skin as he'd dreamed they would be. While he made love to her.

He gripped the arm of the sofa to keep from kissing her again. "Are you in love with him?"

The expression on her face was nothing short of shock. That should have eased his mind, but he needed more.

"In love with him? Special Agent Markus Black? Absolutely not!"

"Then what?"

"I went on a date with him four years ago."

"A date?"

"Yes. And I had coffee with him. That's when I discovered how much I hate coffee."

"Just one date?"

"One was one too many."

Michael opened his mouth to ask her to explain. He suddenly wanted to know every detail about the date. What could possibly have happened that had caused her to not only grow so tense she'd nearly broken his hand, but to stop breathing when she saw the FBI agent?

Even now, as she talked about him, Michael felt her stiffen with tension.

"Do you know what the most aggravating thing is?" Tess asked.

"No, what?"

"I used to think it was knowing that I was just another number in his scrapbook. But now I know that what really bothers me is knowing that he thinks of every woman as a possible number."

"You're certain you're a number?"

"I'm certain I was a number—fifty-two. And all he ever remembers is numbers. He never remembers the women."

Michael shrugged lightly. "I'm not sure I remember every date I went on." Then he grinned wryly. "And I'm sure there are girls out there who went out with me and forgot my name by the next night."

"I'm not one of those girls," Tess said softly. She looked up at him. "Can we stop talking about this? I already feel as I've been wrung through the wringer today."

Talking about it was exactly what Michael wanted to do. What could Markus Black have done on a single date that caused her to react so adversely to him? He wanted to ask but said, "Sure."

She let out a long sigh and dropped her head against his shoulder. "I'm so tired."

He held her closer and liked the way she fit against him. She smelled good, too—clean, fresh and so womanly. "Then just relax, get some rest."

She looked up at him. "You won't leave?"

"I'll stay right here," he promised.

"I'm afraid to go to sleep." She closed her eyes anyway.

"I'll watch over you."

A few moments later, she relaxed in his arms and her breathing grew even. Shadows danced in the candlelight, and Michael held her close. He wanted to shut out the rest of the world and pretend it was just the two of them, but he couldn't ignore the fact that a brutal killer was somewhere out there, perhaps stalking the woman in his arms. He kept telling himself that she was safe here, that the police were outside and he was inside, and the killer couldn't get to her if he wanted to. So why did terror eat at him with cold, unforgiving teeth?

Chapter Five

Michael started awake at the chime of the doorbell. Then he groaned at the morning light that hurt his eyes and muttered, "Well, the power's back on."

Tess was molded to him, and he liked the way her breasts pressed against his chest. Her soft sigh at his words and the way she snuggled closer to him sent heat flowing to his middle. The house was silent, letting him know the rain had stopped. And although he wanted nothing more than to spend the day holding her as he was, there was someone at the door.

He tried to stretch. He half reclined against the arm of the deep sofa. His neck was stiff, and his arm was asleep where Tess rested her head on him. Both his feet were on the coffee table, and now his knees ached when he moved his legs. He looked down and was instantly caught in Tess's gaze. Her eyes were as large as saucers, and she looked like she wanted to jump behind the sofa and hide.

The doorbell chimed again.

"I'll see who it is." He hated to leave her, but he also couldn't stand seeing her terrified and answering the door would put her at ease. Unless, of course, it was some stranger wielding a knife.

"Wait, Michael. What if it's him?"

So she'd had the same thought. "Do you think he'd be kind enough to ring the doorbell?"

"Maybe. He might just be trying to find out who lives here."

That was true, but Michael didn't believe it. He started to remind her that the police were outside, but the doorbell chimed a third time. "I'll look out before I unlock the door. I promise."

He doubted any of the guests were murderers. Yet, as he let them in, he knew Tess wouldn't be at ease with them anyway.

He was about to wish Detective Jake Williams, Agent Markus Black and the other man with them a good morning. Then he knew by their grim expressions that this would be anything but a good morning.

He looked toward the living room doorway and saw Tess standing there. He fought down the urge to tell her to relax, but the tension that filled the room was so thick he could have sliced through it with a knife.

"Sorry about coming by so early." It was Jake who spoke first.

Tess was suddenly cold and fought down a shiver. "You've found another body, haven't you?" she asked, her throat suddenly so tight, her words were hardly more than whispers. When Michael moved closer to her, she gripped his hand tightly.

"Are you Tess Fairmont?" the unknown man in a suit asked.

Tess wanted to throw something at him for not answering her question, yet expecting her to answer his. She wondered if they actually taught a class in arrogance at Quantico. "Yes."

"You're the psychic?" was his next question.

If he asked her to guess his name since she was psychic, she'd probably be arrested for assaulting a police officer. "I've been known to see things at times." She chose her words carefully and ignored Markus Black's stare.

Michael obviously felt the tension that singed through the room and tried to put a damper on it. "Why don't you gentlemen step into the kitchen where I can get you something to drink? Tess and I were about to fix some breakfast."

He tugged on her hand and led her away. The three men had no choice but to follow.

"This is Special Agent Wheston," Jake said once everyone was in the kitchen.

Tess nodded to Wheston, then concentrated on watching Michael when he let go of her hand to reach for the teakettle. The way he tried to keep some normalcy in the situation touched her.

She fought the urge to giggle when he asked, "Are you guys going to eat with us?"

"No." Wheston's voice was clipped.

"Well, I'd offer you all some coffee, but we don't drink coffee here.

Tess couldn't believe how light he managed to keep his

voice. She fought the urge to hug him.

I have juice, tea, milk, and hot chocolate, if that's your drink of choice for the morning."

"Nothing for me, thank you," Markus Black said.

Michael noticed he stared hard at Tess, then pulled out a small notebook and appeared to write something in it.

Agent Wheston wanted nothing either, but Jake accepted a glass of ice water.

Subtly, Michael moved a stool to the other side of the counter for Tess and directed her to it. This way, she'd be in the kitchen area with him and the three lawmen would be on the other side of the counter.

"Do you mind if I ask you a few questions, Ms. Fairmont?" Agent Wheston's voice, although still slightly clipped and somewhat nasally, rang with authority.

"Of course not, as long as you answer mine. Did you find another body or not?"

Much to Tess's surprise, Agent Wheston pulled out an eight-by-ten color photograph of a pretty, young woman with dark hair. He slid it across the counter in Tess's direction. "No, we did not. Do you recognize this woman?"

Tess stared at the picture for a moment. "No. I've never seen her before. She wasn't in any of my visions."

Agent Wheston asked, "Can you state your address for me, please?"

Tess glanced at Michael as if she didn't understand the question. "My address?"

"Would you care to explain what this is about?" Michael asked.

Agent Wheston never took his gaze from Tess. "Just answer the question, please."

"I live at the corner of First Street and Chestnut in Willow," Tess replied, her voice filled with hesitation. She looked at Jake. "Detective Williams knows where I live."

"Your actual address, please, Ms. Fairmont." Agent Wheston persisted.

"What exactly is your role here, Agent Wheston?" Michael asked, his voice tinged with anger.

The man finally looked at Michael. His look said *stay out of this.* "Please, Ms. Fairmont."

"My actual address is 101 West Chestnut. Why?" Tess felt her patience slipping away like a fistful of sand disappearing between her fingers.

Agent Wheston looked squarely at her before he glanced down at the photograph. "This is Madelyn Prange, housewife, mother of three. A soccer mom. She was reported missing yesterday afternoon when she didn't report to the school to pick up her oldest child. There were signs of a struggle at her house. Normally, people aren't considered missing for twenty-four hours, but this report happened to come across Detective Williams's computer because of her address—101 West Chestnut, Oak Park."

A shiver went up Tess's spine. Michael took her hand, and Tess clung to him as she met Jake's gaze. "You think while I was out looking for him yesterday, he was out looking for me?"

"We think that's a definite possibility. This is too much of a coincidence." Jake looked at her with something close to sympathy in his expression.

Tess licked her lips to bring some moisture to her mouth. She'd be eternally thankful that these men had come before she'd eaten breakfast or she'd be tossing it right now.

Jake went on. "As I said, there were obvious signs of a struggle in the living room, and a neighbor saw a dark van in her driveway."

Tess had to close her eyes and swallow hard.

"Did you have any more dreams about him, Tess?"

She shook her head slowly, feeling as if every action she made was underwater. "No."

"Explain your earlier visions to Agent Wheston." It was the first time Agent Black had spoken since declining Michael's offer of a drink.

Tess explained them in as few sentences as possible.

For the first time, Agent Wheston's expression softened. "I work within a special branch of the FBI, Ms. Fairmont. I deal with things that can't be readily explained."

"Like the X-Files?" Tess asked.

He laughed. "No, we're not into anything that dramatic." He sobered then and said, "Special Agent Black called me in on the case, but I wanted to hear about your ability from you. And after what you've just told me, I agree with Detective Williams that Madelyn Prange's disappearance wasn't random. Are you sure there isn't anything else you can tell us that will help us find this guy because his house is empty. It was a rental, and apparently he rented it under an assumed name— John Smith, if you can believe it."

"What did you find at the house?" Tess asked, needing to know.

"Exactly like you said—a dirty fish aquarium, wire and duct tape in the bathroom closet, traces of blood on the dining room chairs and on the floor, evidence on the chairs that he' had the women tied to them, and windows that aren't breakable glass. Is there anything else you can tell us?"

Again, Tess shook her head. "I've told you everything." She glanced down at the photograph and felt bile burn her throat. "He took her, thinking she was me?"

None of the officers confirmed her statement. They didn't have to.

"You haven't 'connected' with him since yesterday afternoon?" Wheston asked.

Tess's stomach burned. "No."

"What about during your vision at the morgue?"

"It was just a—" She searched for the right word "—usual vision. I only saw what the victim saw. Despite the fear I felt, I didn't feel connected to him then."

"Do you know how you connected with him the first time?"

"I don't have a clue. It's never happened before. But then these visions . . ."

"What about them?" he asked, when her voice trailed off.

Tess suddenly felt cold, as cold as she'd felt yesterday when she'd been rain drenched. Michael must have been reading her mind because he set a warm mug of tea in front of her.

She took a sip and said, "I've helped Detective Williams in the past. I always saw bits and pieces and small segments of what happened, but I've never had anything as clear and vivid or as long as these visions."

"Why do you think you're so in tune with him?" Agent Wheston asked.

She shrugged. "I have no idea. Maybe the stars are in the right alignment. Or maybe the pollution wasn't so bad this week. Or perhaps the cell phone towers are putting out extra signals. Maybe it's the energy from the storm or the rain." She looked directly at Agent Wheston. "Or maybe he's just a more horrible killer and he puts out different—even stronger—vibes than other murderers."

She paused and took a heavy breath. "I can tell you that I don't like what's happening. I don't like him invading my space any more than he probably likes me invading his. And it eats at my gut to know that some poor, innocent woman has to suffer because of me."

Michael placed one hand on her shoulder and squeezed her hand with the other as he said softly, "This is not your fault, Tess."

Agent Wheston offered a quick, small smile. "We aren't blaming you, Ms. Fairmont. We're just trying to get as much information as we can so we can stop this man before he hurts someone else."

Tess had to clear her throat. "I've told you everything I know."

"And you're sure you have no idea how you connected with him?"

Tess reminded herself he was really trying to help these women, just as she was, but it didn't make repeating her answers any easier. She told herself she should be glad she could do something. And she should be glad everyone believed her. But not having any more answers frustrated the hell out of her.

She took a deep breath and forced some patience into her voice. "No, I don't. If I did, I'd do it again so I could tell him he has the wrong woman and maybe he'd let her go." She knew that was a long shot, given this killer's record, but Tess could hope.

"Do you think you could connect with him again, perhaps

enough to see where he's gone or where he's taken his victims?"

Tess shook her head, wishing she had a better answer. "Since I don't know how I connected with him in the first place, I have no idea how to do it again."

"I don't think we need to rehash this," Michael put in.

Tess was so thankful for his interruption, she could have kissed him.

"Tess has answered all your questions" he continued. "So unless you care to join us for some pancakes and bacon . . ." Michael let the sentence die, but it was clearly a dismissal.

Agent Wheston's calm expression never changed. Jake looked clearly relieved, and Agent Black's brows drew closer together, as if he couldn't believe Michael would have the gall to so boldly send them on their way.

Finally, Agent Wheston said, "Please let us know if you have any more visions."

"Of course," Tess said.

The two agents left, but Jake lingered in the kitchen. "I'm sorry about that, Tess."

"It's not your fault." Tess had to force her words through a painfully tight throat.

"If I could have warned you, I would have. But when your address came across my desk with a different name, I had to check it out, and I was obligated to call Markus Black. He just showed up with Wheston this morning and said they wanted to see you. They wouldn't let me call ahead."

"I understand," she said.

"I'll be in touch."

He turned and headed toward the door, but he stopped in his tracks when she said, "I want to go to her house."

He turned back to her. "What?"

"The woman he thought was me—I want to go to her house."

"Do you think you'd see something?"

Tess shrugged. "I usually only see things when I touch dead people, but sometimes I feel things." She didn't explain that she usually felt things like goodness when she touched anything belonging to Michael, or illness, like when she'd touched the salt shaker at the diner. "I've also never been connected like this to anyone before. Maybe we'll get lucky if I touch something he touched. It's better than doing nothing or just waiting for him to do something horrible, right?"

Jake gave her a small smile and indicated the door with a nod. "Let me go out and talk with them. While we make some plans, you'll have the chance to get something to eat."

Eat? Tess thought as she watched him leave. She wasn't sure she'd ever be able to eat again.

"I probably should have shown Jake out, but I didn't think it was worth letting go of your hand." Michael said, giving her hand a squeeze.

"Thank you." Tess's words were soft. She slid off the stool and into his arms, and for a few moments, the rest of the world went away and she felt at peace.

But that peace was shortlived because Jake suddenly cleared his throat. Tess turned and met his gaze, but didn't move away from Michael. She nearly smiled at the idea that Michael didn't let her go, either. In fact, she thought he held her closer. She felt his heart beating and she fought the urge to lean her head on his shoulder.

"I spoke with Black and Wheston, as well as the cops in Oak Park. They said if you want to check out the house, we can do that," Jake informed them. "How soon can you be ready?"

Tess looked at Michael and felt something like a mental message pass through her.

"Ten minutes," Tess replied. "But on the way, I need to stop at my house and pick up some clean clothes and personal items."

"I don't think that will be a problem."

"And I'll drive her," Michael put in.

Jake didn't look as if he liked that idea, but he didn't argue. "We'll be outside."

"We'll be out in a few minutes."

The kitchen was silent again with Jake's departure. Tess gave in to the urge and rested her head on Michael's shoulder, relishing in the safe feeling of Michael's arms around her. She breathed in a deep breath and was filled with the subtle scent of soap and Michael's slightly woodsy, outdoorsy scent.

She looked up to find him looking down at her.

"I hope you don't mind that I offered to drive or demanded that we stop by your place."

She smiled. It was so easy to smile when she was with him, no matter how much terror churned through her. "No, it's fine, as long as you're there with me."

He nodded, but he studied her, his expression both worried and concerned. "You're sure you want to do this?"

"I'm pretty sure I *don't* want to do it. This man terrifies me, and the thought that he wanted me badly enough that he mistook someone else for me and didn't even take the time to confirm that he had the right person turns my insides to jelly. But I'll do whatever I can to help this woman and all the others he has with him."

He still looked worried, so she smiled at him again. "I think it's pretty gallant of you to offer to drive considering this is only our second date."

Michael grinned. "This has to be the longest second date I've ever had."

Tess couldn't help chuckling. "Me, too."

"And except for the lunatic trying to grab you, I'm having a great time."

"Me, too. Of course, I'd be winning if we were playing rummy."

"In your dreams," he muttered.

"Oh, if my dreams could be that boring."

Suddenly, without warning, his mouth on hers, his kiss hot and filled with longing.

Oh, this man could kiss! Her lips, her tongue, and even her soul felt ravished. Her lips tingled while the rest of her quivered. Beneath it all, she still wanted more. Why him? Was there really such a thing as soul mates—one heart, two people? Was that why she longed to sink to the floor and take Michael with her when, until now, a man's closeness had made her want to run away?

Her nipples were instantly alive and hard and pressing

against his chest. The rest of her body followed suit and pressed against him.

And as if in reply to her body's need, Tess felt every contour of him—the hard muscles of his thighs and the flatness of his belly. He took a breath and his chest tickled her breasts. He slid his hands down her back and Tess could have sworn he left a trail of fire in his wake. At her derriere, he pressed his palms against each cheek and forced her pelvis against his.

Tess let out a groan, and the sound seemed to bring them both back to reality, because Michael said, "I could tell Jake we need a half hour." His words were both breathy and harsh.

Tess licked her lips and couldn't ignore the way they felt tender and swollen from his kiss. "We'd better not."

"Why not?"

"I think we'll need longer than a half hour."

He grinned at her. "You can't blame a guy for trying." His next kiss was quick, but held a promise of more to come. "Let me fix you a bagel to go."

"Sounds great. Nobody else fixes a bagel as good as you do," she teased.

"It's all in the toaster."

Tess smiled, but she hoped that the bagel would stay where it should.

Chapter Six

The ride to Tess's house was uneventful. Uneventful, if Tess could forget there was a killer searching for her because she'd been so unlucky to somehow connect with him. Uneventful, if Tess could disregard the questions Agent Wheston continued to ask from the backseat. He had insisted on riding with her and neither Tess nor Michael or even Jake could deter him. His nasally voice raked on her nerves. Tess did her best to ignore that part since she knew he was trying to find answers that would help save these kidnapped women.

Tess sat in the front and turned to look back at him a few times. Each time, his soft, easy expression barely changed. Tess thought he should play professional poker. No one would ever know what he thought. She knew she certainly didn't. Michael held her hand as he drove. His touch kept her grounded and feeling safe.

She stared out the windshield at other cars that passed them as they followed Jake and Agent Black. Where was everyone going? To doctors' appointments? To the grocery store? Wonderful, normal everyday activities. She bet no one else was going to the home of a missing woman.

As they headed north, the sun gave way now and then to building clouds, and before long, Michael was forced to run the wipers as a soft mist fell.

"Were you ever in a coma?" Agent Wheston asked.

"No."

"Have you ever been abused or experienced any type of head trauma?"

At the question, her seat belt choked her. The visions themselves were abuse enough. The years of being called a freak were abusive. Michael must have sensed her discomfort because he squeezed her hand. His hand was warm, and she concentrated on that warmth as she forced out, "No."

"You said your first episode came when you touched your deceased grandmother?"

Episode? He made it sound as if they were talking about a television program. This was her life, without commercials, without sponsorship, without the opportunity to change the channel or edit out the bad stuff. Too bad, because if she could, she would certainly edit out this murderer.

"Yes." Her answer was barely a whisper.

Michael cast another quick glance at her and shifted his hand to lace their fingers together. She tightened her fingers against his, imagining him enfolding her in his arms and bathing her in his warmth.

"Do you know what determines the intensity of your visions?" Wheston asked, interrupting her daydream.

Tess was quiet for a long moment as she considered his question. "I've often thought it's because of how close I feel to the victims, but now I'm not sure. I was very close to my grandmother, as well as my uncle who killed her. In the past, I felt as if I've known some of the victims when I've helped Jake, but I think that's because I had the chance to meet family members before I touched the victim."

"What about this latest series of murders? Do you think you know one of the victims?"

Tess shook her head slowly and concentrated on the tingle Michael's hand sent up her arm. "I don't know any of them." It was the truth, but she also felt as if her words were a lie because she certainly knew them after she lived their last moments.

"What about their murderer? Is it possible you know him?"

She nearly shivered and squeezed Michael's hand as she turned slightly in her seat again to look squarely at Agent Wheston. "That's not an easy question to answer. I feel like I do know him, but I think it's because his victims know him."

"Agent Black says that's not possible."

A memory touched Tess—white, hot, sudden, and intense, the memory of Markus Black telling Tess she tasted like cotton candy. She swallowed past the sudden lump in her throat and forced that memory away. "All I know is that when I have the visions, I feel as if they know him."

"I know you said they only called him by his first name, but were there any nicknames used?"

"No. Just Raymond." The bagel Michael had fixed her had tasted delicious, but now it felt like a brick in the bottom of her stomach.

The car's temperature was comfortable, yet Tess felt cold and clammy. She knew, however, that turning up the heater wouldn't help.

Agent Wheston's words grew soft. "Do you feel their pain?"

Tess knew exactly what he meant, and she tried to decide if she wanted to answer. Finally, she decided that he knew everything else about her, so there was no reason to lie. "Yes, I feel what he does to them."

Agent Wheston was quiet for a long moment, as if he needed to digest everything she'd told him.

Thankfully, they reached Tess's house a few minutes later. She and Michael waited in the car with Agent Wheston while Jake and Agent Black checked out the house. When they gave the all-clear sign, Tess climbed out of the car and breathed in a deep breath of moist air. Had it only been two days since she stood in her front yard and stared at her house, longing to fill it with a family? She swallowed hard, forcing down the cold, sick feeling that the worst murderer she'd ever envisioned had almost found his way into what she always felt was her safe haven. He just hadn't been as lucky to find her as she had him. But why?

That question raised several others. Would he recognize her if he saw her? Since he'd gone to the wrong address and taken Madelyn Prange, she assumed he wouldn't, but that might not be true. He may have taken Madelyn simply because she'd seen him. But if he didn't recognize her, then how had he connected with her? Did he somehow sense her within his victims, or did he see her separate from them?

Unfortunately, she didn't have the answers to any of her questions. But regardless of how he'd sensed her, she obviously worried him. Why else would he have gone after her so quickly?

Michael suddenly stood beside her. "You can wait out here if you like, and I can pack up some clothes for you."

His offer touched her heart. He was so observant, so in tune with her.

"What, and let you check out my underwear drawer?" she asked softly, trying to lighten her own dark mood.

He quirked a brow at her. "If you go in, can I still check out your underwear drawer?"

She glanced up and saw Agent Wheston, who stood several yards away, looking at them as if he'd heard their conversation. Tess had the sudden urge to burst out laughing at the thought. This must be how hysteria felt, she decided. One minute, she wanted to curl up in a corner; the next she wanted to laugh wildly.

Michael must have sensed her underlying hysteria because he put his arm around her and led her toward her front door, stating lightly, "Nice place you have here."

Tess smiled at him. "How do you do that?"

His body brushed against her side as they moved together. "Do what?"

"Manage to sound as if I simply invited you over for lunch, like there isn't someone running around out there who would like to stab me with his knife?"

"It's easier when I touch you," Michael stated.

"Please don't stop touching me," Tess said softly as they reached her front door, and she saw Jake waiting just inside her foyer.

"I won't."

He kept his promise, even staying with her in her bedroom while she threw a few sets of clothes, another pair of shoes and some toiletries into a duffel bag. But he didn't joke any more about her underwear drawer, and oddly, that made her feel sad.

"You're wound tighter than a drum." Michael's words sounded unusually loud in the bedroom.

Tess paused and looked at him. "The house is so silent."

Michael looked around, as if confused. "Isn't it usually?"

"Not this quiet. It's unnerving." She quickly piled her belongings into the bag and zipped it shut. She met his gaze. "And it still feels . . . dirty, as if he's been here even though I know that he went to the Prange house instead. I might have to get new furniture when this is over." Assuming I can even live here, she added silently, then said aloud, "Do you think I have time to change into my own clothes? Not that yours aren't comfortable, but I look a little, well, baggy."

He grinned at her. "You look great in baggy, but I'm sure you can have as much time as you need to change. I'll be right outside the door."

He walked toward the open door, and she said, "Michael?" He turned back to her, and she nervously swiped her hands against the sweat pants she wore. "Please don't go. Just close the door and turn your back. I don't want to be alone in here."

His expression grew serious. "Do you really feel as if he's been here?"

She looked warily around the room. "I don't know. Maybe it's just the remnants of my dream. I just don't want to be alone. I want to change fast and get out of here."

Michael nodded, closed the door and turned to face it.

Tess couldn't help admiring the back of him. Lean but muscular hips and thighs. Nice butt. Broad shoulders. No wonder she felt his strength when he held her. He was all strong male.

She quickly slipped out of his sweats and replaced them with clean undies, a pair of comfortable jeans, and a tee shirt that said: *What happens in Vegas, stays in Vegas.*

"I'm ready."

Michael turned and his gaze swept down her. He grinned again. "Vegas, huh?"

"My brother lives out there, and I go to visit him. Have you ever been to Vegas?"

"No, but I've always wanted to." He picked up her bag while she slipped on a hoodie and zipped it up. While he carried her bag to the front door, Tess moved to the kitchen to grab a couple of boxes of flavored tea bags to take to Michael's house.

She opened the kitchen cabinet and pulled out the boxes. When she closed the cabinet, she was startled to find Agent Black standing there.

"Agent Black?" She found it impossible to keep her words

from sounding tight when she addressed him.

He didn't answer but stared at her. Tess started to turn away, but he stopped her by placing a hand on her arm. She looked down at his hand, barely able to tolerate his touch.

"You know, Tess," he said, "sooner or later, we might have to talk."

With his touch on her arm, she felt so much—his cool, professional exterior that he allowed others to see mixed with the dark part he worked so hard to keep hidden. "We don't have anything to talk about except this case," she said, working to keep her voice even and light.

"Four years ago, you walked out on me without a word, even refused my phone calls. I deserve to know why."

She looked down at his hand again before meeting his gaze. "I refused to be number fifty-two," she said.

"What?"

"That's what I would have been, right, if I had stayed—number fifty-two?"

His silence was more than an answer. "How?" he began.

"You touched me. You kissed me. Sometimes people don't have be dead in order for me to see things."

She never looked away from him. He was the first to look away, and he released her arm as if touching her burned him.

Tess took the opportunity to pick up the two small boxes of tea bags and turn away. She stopped short at the sight of Michael in the kitchen doorway. Then she moved to him and took his hand. "Ready?"

"I guess."

It was evident he questioned what he had just seen or what he might have overheard. At his car, he opened the passenger door for her. And he was kind enough to not ask any questions about Markus Black.

"Are you okay?" he asked

She climbed into the front seat. "Yep."

He closed her door and moved to put her bag in the trunk. Then he climbed in, too. Agent Wheston followed suit and climbed into the back, and they moved on toward Oak Park.

* * * *

With its beautiful architecture of arched doorways, brick designs, balconies and quaint setting, Oak Park was picturesque. Despite the dreary day, people moved on the sidewalks, the trees showed a hint of spring color, and the houses appeared well cared for with balanced landscaping and tiled drives. Yet, to Tess, it felt surreal. She kept thinking she was in the middle of a terrible nightmare, and sooner or later—hopefully sooner—she would wake up.

But as much as she wished it, she knew she wasn't dreaming. It disconcerted her that the world moved on despite the fact that a killer was out there murdering women, despite the fact children were without their mother because Tess had somehow connected to that same killer.

Michael parked behind Jake and Agent Black in a driveway not far from the deserted ice rink. The house was a modest gray brick two story with an arched front door and brick steps leading the way to it. The numbers 101 graced the door, looking like ceramic stairsteps. The same house number and address as her own. As Tess stared at the numbers, she thought she'd have this same odd sense of déjà vu if she were reading an obituary with her name in the headline.

Tess continued to stare at the house and didn't make a move to get out of the car even though she knew she had to. After all, they'd come here at her request.

Michael looked over at her. "Tess?"

"It resembles my house a little," she said. "The gray bricks aren't too different in color than the stone at my house and the arched doorway looks about the same. I kept hoping it would be totally different, that somehow the killer just got a glimpse of the street name and number. But even though this house is much bigger, I can see where he might have confused it with my house. Even the plants outside the front door look a little like mine."

Michael let out a heavy breath. "Tess, this is not your fault."

"Of course it's my fault. If I hadn't somehow connected with him, he would have never come after me and taken this woman by mistake."

"If you hadn't connected with him, we wouldn't know

anything at all about him." He covered her hand with his. "If you don't want to go in there, you don't have to. I can take you home, and we'll plant flowers in the yard or something."

Tess closed her eyes, imagining something as mindless as planting flowers. Creating beauty sounded wonderful, but it wouldn't be enough to erase the terror this killer had brought into her world.

"There is no way I can sit back and do nothing." She opened her eyes and looked at Michael. "Even if you do need flowers planted. So let's just get his over with."

She and Michael climbed out. Michael met her gaze over the roof of the car and Tess wondered how she could be so far away from him and still feel close, still feel his warmth touch her like rays of the sun. After he lightly slammed his door, he rounded the car and joined her. She grasped Michael's hand firmly and they followed Agent Wheston toward the front door.

The air was muggy and heavy with moisture. Still, Tess shivered.

The man who opened the door after Agent Wheston rang the bell was tall and strong, and his hair was neat and golden. His eyes were dark brown. He wore slacks and a white, button-down shirt. The sleeves were rolled up nearly to his elbows.

Yet, as handsome as he was, it wasn't the man who caused Tess's breath to catch. It was the baby girl in his arms. She had curly ringlets of red-blond hair, fat cheeks and eyes that matched the man's who held her. She couldn't have been more than a year old, and she stared at the people on her doorstep as if to say, "Okay, where's my mommy?"

Then a whimper from closer to the floor caught Tess's attention. There, holding onto the man's leg was another child, a boy of perhaps three or four years old, a small replica of the man.

Tess thought her knees might buckle. It was one thing to know someone was missing, but it was much harder to face when you saw all that was left behind. These children needed their mother. And thanks to Tess, they might never see her again.

"Officer Williams? Agent Black? Agent Wheston?" The

man's voice was rich and deep, and yet it sounded hollow at the same time. Dark circles floated beneath his eyes. Had he been up all night crying over his missing wife? Or had he merely been up all night with kids who were crying for their missing mother? His gaze moved suddenly to Tess. "Is this the psychic you called about?"

Tess could barely meet his gaze. She supposed she should be upset that she'd been called a psychic, but what other label could she have been given? Visionary of the dead? She didn't think that one would be readily accepted by a husband with a baby in his arms.

"This is Tess Fairmont, Mr. Prange." It was Jake who introduced her. "And this is Dr. Adams."

"Is he a psychic, too?" Mr. Prange studied Tess for a moment before turning his attention to Michael.

"He's sort of Ms. Fairmont's helper," Jake replied without hesitation. "Can we come in?"

Prange moved out of the way, shuffling in a stiff but patient way because of the child who gripped his leg. The five of them filed into the foyer. It was probably an elegant house, but children inhabited it, so it looked more lived in with toys scattered around the floor, a few dirty spots on the carpet, and a quilt protecting the sofa. There was also the subtle scent of baby powder. To Tess, it was an inviting home, one where the door opened easily to friends who understood that toys too soon disappeared and babies grew up too quickly. It was the type of home she'd love to have.

An older woman seemingly appeared out of nowhere, stretching out her arms and saying, "Give her to me, Darrin." She easily took the baby from Prange.

"This is my mother, Sandra," Darrin Prange said.

They murmured greetings.

Darrin looked at them with narrowed eyes. "Do you really think your coming here will help? Shouldn't you be out looking for my wife?"

Tess had started to wonder the same thing after she'd stepped into the house and felt nothing but pain and grief, a sense of loss combined with worry and fatigue. Sandra took the baby out of the room. Tess watched them leave, noticing then that another child, a girl of about nine or ten stood silent and still in the doorway. She watched them with large, round brown eyes. Like the baby and the little boy, this sad-eyed girl was beautiful. She was also old enough to understand that bad things happened to people, and she obviously missed her mother.

Another wave of guilt hit Tess. She had to help this family. It was because of her these children were missing their mother.

Jake cleared his throat before telling Darrin Prange, "Right now, we're doing everything we can."

"Of course, you are," Darrin replied, his voice laced with sarcasm.

Jake leaned close and quietly spoke in Tess's ear. "See what you can do."

She slipped her hand from Michael's and moved away toward the living room. She met Darrin's sorrowful gaze. "Where was your wife when she was taken?"

"You're the psychic, don't you know?" It was obvious from Darrin's sarcastic tone that he didn't believe in her talent or want her here.

"Every piece of information helps," she replied softly.

Darrin glared at her, but she met his gaze steadily. Finally, he let out a heavy breath. "There were broken picture frames and that funky thing she dusts with on the floor in the living room."

Tess walked into the living room, trying to force herself to relax. Wasn't that how she had the best visions, when she was relaxed? Suddenly, she wasn't so sure it made a difference. She really had no control over the visions. They simply came when they wanted.

There was no glass or funky dusting thing on the floor, but there were two picture frames on the mantle that had no glass. Tess took a deep breath and touched them. Then she took one in her hands, concentrating on forming a vision, just as she did when she took a victim's hand.

She stood still and quiet, concentrating on her breathing as she stared at the picture in the glassless frame. The five people in the photograph stared back at her, their faces taken up with big smiles—Darrin, his three children, a woman with dark hair and an easy smile. They looked happy and carefree sitting in the front yard of this house. The season was fall, with colorful leaves scattered around them.

But no matter how hard she concentrated, she felt nothing, saw nothing. What good was this "gift" if she couldn't use it when she needed to? she thought in frustration.

With gentle care, she replaced the frame on the mantle and reached for another one, this one with glass in it. She now stared down at a photograph of Darrin and Madelyn Prange, although both looked a bit younger than the family picture.

No vision came to her. But something else did. It was that locker room smell she recognized from the killer's house. It mixed with that odd sense of unclean that Tess had felt after she'd connected with him. The same feeling she'd experienced when she was in his house.

She closed her eyes and lightly ran her fingertips along the edge of the frame. There was no mistake, the killer had touched this frame. He had been in this room. She knew his scent couldn't linger, couldn't still be here, and yet she could still smell him. Just as she recognized the killer's lingering essence, she realized that her visions were filled with sensations, smells, and even sounds. Now, when she thought of the killer's house, she remembered hearing the pump filtering the fish aquarium. The memory of that scraping sound as he sharpened a knife . . .

"Are you really psychic?"

Darrin had spoken from right behind her. Tess started and nearly dropped the photograph. She'd been so busy concentrating on trying to pick up something that might lead them to the killer that she hadn't realized the man had approached her.

"Something like that." Tess didn't put down the photograph nor did she look up at him. She didn't want to seem unkind or cold, but she didn't want to break her concentration.

"And this is more than just a missing person, isn't it?" There was pain in Darrin's voice. "Otherwise, the police would wait twenty-four hours before even looking into it, wouldn't they? I've heard of those other murders. You think the man who took Maddie is that killer, don't you?"

For the first time, Agent Wheston spoke from the doorway. "If you could please give her some space, Mr. Prange. Rest assured, we're checking every avenue."

Tess was glad for Agent Wheston's interruption. Darrin Prange's whirlwind of fear and grief left her with a slight headache at the base of her skull. After another deep breath, she looked down at the photograph again.

"What the hell kind of answer is that? Do you even have any clues? What other 'avenues' have you checked out?"

"Mr. Prange?" Markus Black said. "May I speak with you in the kitchen?"

Darrin glared at Markus and looked as if he'd refuse, but then he suddenly deflated like a pricked balloon and nodded.

Tess watched them go. The little girl still stared at them from the doorway. Tess met her gaze. She looked like her mother.

"You're going to find my mom, aren't you?" The child's voice was small but strong.

"We're going to do our best," Tess replied softly. She didn't dare make a promise she might not be able to keep. She looked back at the photograph and placed three fingers against the glass.

Yes, he'd touched this picture, and he'd spoke to Madelyn.

As soon as she realized that, the vision hit her. Madelyn was on the floor, on her back, the feather duster falling from her grasp slightly. He'd done something to her—injected her with a drug? Tess wasn't sure.

And what did he say? Something about if her husband knew she'd actually spent the day before with him. It wasn't so much what he said as the way he said it that convinced Tess that he'd thought Madelyn was her.

Tess carefully replaced the photograph and crouched down, tentatively putting both palms on the floor as she worked to ignore the little's girl's hopeful, trusting look as she watched Tess.

She felt the child's feelings almost as strongly, if not stronger than, the remnant's of Madelyn's and her kidnapper's and

Darrin's. The young girl mentally pleaded for Tess to find her mother and bring her home.

The wood floor was cool beneath her touch, but then like the hand of a victim, it grew warm. Unfortunately, no vision came, yet the heat gave her clues.

Yes, Madelyn had lain here, conscious but stunned or drugged, unable to move.

Yes, her kidnapper, the murderer of several women, had spoken to her.

Yes, Madelyn's fear was overwhelming, but it was for the baby girl who slept in her crib upstairs.

And then Tess heard him say, "Does your wonderful husband know what a slut you are? Does he know you creep into other people's homes and spy on them?"

As he spoke, the killer's voice seemed to scream in her head. It hurt Tess's ears and her mild headache turned into a full, throbbing pain that forced her to close her eyes as the killer said, "I don't know how you found me, but while I'm taking the gang west, you can tag along and camp and hike with the rest of us!"

Madelyn Prange stared up at him in terror and whimpered, "I don't know what you're talking about!"

She doesn't look anything like me, Tess thought, but he still thought she was me. It proved that even though he'd somehow connected with her enough to see her address, he hadn't seen her face.

The voice had stopped, and Tess pulled away from the floor. There wasn't even any lingering echo of his voice in the room, but she nearly moaned at the assault of emotions that continued to rake through her. Terror, pain from hitting the floor, frustration at the inability to move, worry over the baby and the children at school . . . Tess felt the aftermath of every emotion Madelyn Prange had felt and decided she could have been run over by a truck and felt less. She couldn't fight down the shudder that moved through her. All she wanted was to get out of this house, curl up somewhere, close her eyes to the horror, and sleep for three or four days.

Tess looked at Wheston. "He's heading west. He's still

talking about camping and hiking. He's got a definite destination in mind. Maybe you should check out campgrounds and stores that sell outdoor gear."

"Why would he talk about camping or hiking? Campgrounds aren't open yet," Agent Wheston pointed out.

Tess had to work to keep from laughing, knowing it would be hysterical laughter. "I don't know, but since he's not playing by any rules, I doubt that will stop him." Then she moved to the door. She had to get out of here before her knees gave out.

At the front door, Darrin Prange stopped her. "Did he hurt her? Could you see if he hurt her?"

Tess stared at him for a long moment, as if drugging her and taking her from her home, away from her obviously loving husband and children wasn't enough to cause pain. But she understood his question. "He drugged her so she couldn't fight him. But, no, he did nothing else that I can see besides carry her out to his van."

"So she was still alive when he took her from here?" Darrin swallowed hard enough that Tess saw his throat move. He was grasping for straws, searching for hope. She couldn't blame him.

"Yes." She was being honest. She only hoped this psychopath didn't kill Madelyn Prange out of anger when he discovered he had the wrong woman.

Once she was in the car, Tess leaned her head against the headrest, still drained. Michael didn't grasp her hand, but he did reach across the seat and place his hand over hers like a cozy blanket.

From the backseat, Agent Wheston fired questions at her. Tess didn't have to open her eyes to know he was writing in his notebook. She heard the scribble of his pen on the paper between answers.

"What did you see?

"What did you feel?

"Did you smell any unusual odors?

"Did you hear actual voices?

"Did you feel hot or cold or numb or clammy?

"Did you feel as if you floated over your body?

"Was it like you were the cameraman in a movie or were you actually one of the actors?"

Before now, Tess hadn't realized how the sound of his voice raked on her nerves. Her head still pounded, and his barrage of questions was making it worse.

"Can't you see she needs a few moments to recoup? Give it a rest, Agent Wheston, or you can get out and walk." Michael's voice was calm but firm in his threat.

Tess nearly laughed. She could just imagine how it would look if Michael booted Agent Wheston out of the car. Maybe then she'd have some peace. Right then, her entire insides quivered, and if she had to stand up, her legs probably wouldn't hold her. If she didn't know better, she'd think a million tiny spiders crawled through her body making her feel a lot like the antsy feeling she'd had after connecting with the killer. She was glad Michael continued to rest his hand over hers so she didn't have to see or feel her hands shaking. She wondered if the killer felt anything right now. She certainly hoped she was able to shred his nerves as easily as he did hers.

"Are you okay?" Michael's words were soft, and the pressure of his hand increased.

Tess had to clear her throat before she could reply. "I don't think I'm ever going to be okay again. I think I'm going to just keep quivering and shaking until I break into a million pieces, if the top of my head doesn't pop off first."

"I'll take you home and you can relax, let go of all of this for a while."

"That sounds like a wonderful idea, mixed with some strong headache medicine."

"And maybe something good to eat, too."

"I don't know if that's such a great idea."

"Oh, I don't know. Chocolate has a way of working miracles sometimes." Tess didn't have to look at him to know he grinned. She felt it. "I need to stop for gas, though. Is that all right?"

She finally looked at him. "Of course."

Michael glanced into the rearview mirror. "Agent Wheston, let Jake know we're stopping, would you?"

Agent Wheston pulled out his cell phone and called Agent

Black to confirm.

Tess leaned toward Michael. "Do you think they have to confirm with one another before they go the bathroom?" She spoke softly, but didn't really care if Agent Wheston heard her.

"Probably." Michael grinned again, and this time Tess saw it.

Agent Wheston said. "Just pull into the next station."

Michael did, maneuvering smoothly across traffic.

"Tess, do you feel as if you connected with the killer when you were in the Prange house?" Agent Wheston asked.

"No," Tess took a deep breath, wishing her headache would lighten up. It didn't. "No, what I felt at the Prange house was nothing like what I felt yesterday. But I do feel exhausted and antsy, like I did when I connected with him."

"Anything else out of the ordinary?" Agent Wheston asked.

"The smell," Tess confessed as Michael turned off the engine.

"Smell?" Michael asked.

"I keep smelling the killer's house. It's like I can't get it out of my nose. Even at the Prange house, I could smell him, like he was still there," she explained. "And my head hurts really bad."

"Do you often get headaches after your visions?" Agent Wheston asked.

"Yes, but never like this." Tess rubbed the back of her neck.

Michael looked over the seat at Wheston. "Do you think you could go in and get her something for her headache while I fill the tank?"

"I'll be right back." Agent Wheston got out of the car at the same time Michael did.

Tess watched him stride toward the station's quick mart. She glanced out the back window at Michael, who opened the gas tank cover. He smiled at her through the window before he turned and reached for the pump.

Tess offered him a small smile. Then she took a deep breath and closed her eyes, forcing herself to relax. More than just her head, her entire body ached, as if her experience at the

Prange home had somehow left her beaten.

She closed out the noise around her, the muffled sounds of traffic, the radio playing in the car two pumps away, the slam of a car door. It all faded into silence. Then she thought she felt and heard the rumble of the engine—strange, Michael didn't have the car running. He wasn't finished pumping the gas.

The smell touched her—that odor that made her wrinkle her nose, the unclean, locker room smell.

When she finally opened her eyes, she was no longer in Michael's car . . .

Chapter Seven

Tess let out a startled cry when she opened her eyes to find she was no longer in Michael's car. Nor was she in the gas station waiting for Michael to finish pumping gas.

She was so deep within a vision, she was sitting in the front seat of a moving van.

And if it had been anything more than a vision, if she were really sitting in the van's front seat, she might have slid off the seat or even slipped into a different, less comfortable position. Or perhaps she might have curled into a fetal position and closed her eyes against the horror that suddenly gripped her.

She'd only meant to close her eyes for a moment, only meant to force her aching limbs to relax and hope that her headache might fade. And somehow she'd again connected to the murderer.

She turned and found she was mere few feet from him, with no other room in which to hide or escape. In this dream state, everything was incredibly enhanced. Her terror sent her heart racing at a dangerous speed. She felt as if millions of tiny spiders crawled all over her. The light, despite the clouds that hid the sun, hurt her eyes. She tried to swallow, but the lump in her throat felt as if she'd managed to swallow a golf ball.

And that smell . . .

Her stomach did a somersault. That locker room smell touched her like a huge, icy claw. And his closeness sent terror through her so strong she thought she might be sick to her stomach.

In the driver's seat, Raymond jerked toward her. Then he slammed on the brakes. Objects in the van—an empty paper cup, a wadded paper bag from a fast food restaurant, the CD case on the console between them—all flew forward. Oddly, of all the things that touched Tess's senses, the feel of motion did not. She didn't feel the seat she sat in or any sense that she was sliding forward. Nor did she feel a seatbelt.

"What the hell?" He turned to her.

There was no longer any question of whether or not he could see her. He looked right at her.

"You are there, aren't you? I can barely see you, but I know you're there. And how can you be there if you're back in the back of the van with the rest of them? Unless the one I have back there is the wrong woman!"

Tess tried to concentrate. He still wasn't certain who she was.

"Tell me how you do this!" he ranted at her.

Tess had no idea how she did this, but she couldn't let him know that. It would be to her advantage if he thought she could do it anytime, anywhere. But could he hear her if she spoke? There was only one way to find out.

"It doesn't matter," she said.

"Yeah, right. I might not be able to see you as well as I feel you, but at least I'm able to touch you." He reached out and slapped her face.

Tess might not feel the seat, but she felt the raw burn of his fingers. Yet, there was no sound from the slap. How was she connecting to him like this?

She had to think of something quick. She couldn't allow him to hit her or hurt her further, especially when she had no idea how to end this vision "Don't do that again." She forced every bit of hard authority she could muster into her voice.

"Or what? You'll cast a spell on me, because I'm thinking you must be some sort of a damned witch to do what you can do."

"Do you want to test me?" She certainly hoped he didn't, and, thank heavens, he hesitated.

Tess didn't know how long this would last, and she needed as much information and she could gather before it ended. "That's a smart move, not putting me to the test." She turned slightly and looked into the back of the van. With no windows, there was little light, but she quickly counted five women back there, on the floor, either forced to lie down or drugged, their arms bound behind them. And she thought she glimpsed Madelyn Prange's dark hair. Thankfully, it looked as if all of them were still alive.

"You're right. The woman you took yesterday is the wrong woman," she said, turning back to face him.

"Oh, I could pretty well figure that out for myself since you're sitting in my front seat. First you invade my house, then you suddenly show up here like some angel able to swoop down on me."

"Or worse." She tried matching the sarcasm in his voice, hoping it would make him think she could do something bad to him if she decided to do so.

A car sped by them, and the van rocked with its air current. Tess looked up, but didn't recognize the highway. She saw a mile marker, a Marla's Diner, and endless pavement. The car that passed them was a red Jeep.

"The woman you kidnapped yesterday—you let her go safe and sound or I'll be back again, and there won't be any question about testing me. You won't pass, I promise."

He grinned at her. "Not a strong enough witch to make me let them all go, huh?

Tess looked at him squarely. She took in every aspect of his face, every line, every acne scar. She planned to give Jake more than a simple sketch. And the last thing she wanted to do was push him too far. "Let Madelyn Prange go, safely, and we'll discuss the others later."

"And if I don't?"

"Since you have no idea how I'm doing this, you also have no idea what else I can do."

"Fine!" he yelled. "I'll let her go."

"Safely."

"Safely," he confirmed. "Now get the hell out of my van."

"Why do you have the others?" Tess had to push.

"The others deserve to be punished." He slapped her again, as if to make his point. She felt the pain rake through her entire body, not just her cheek. She closed her eyes and told herself he really couldn't hurt her because she wasn't here. This had to be a figment of her imagination—and his.

Suddenly, she heard her name from far away. "Tessssss . . ."

There was pressure against her arm, and something warm

touched her hand. Suddenly she opened her eyes, and she was back in Michael's car. Michael leaned over her, his expression worried. Her hand was in his—the warmth she'd felt. With his other hand, he gripped her shoulder which was the pressure she'd felt. "Tess?"

Tess pulled away, slid out of her seatbelt, opened the door and heaved. Nothing came up, but she thought she might suffocate before she was able to catch her breath again.

Michael was suddenly kneeling in front of her, the knees of his jeans probably getting wet and dirty from the gas station's damp concrete. "Tess, what just happened? What happened to you?"

"It was astral projection." Agent Wheston spoke quietly from behind Michael where he stood holding a bottle of water. "I've heard of it, but until now, I'd never seen it."

"I certainly never want to see it again," Tess said in a gasp.

Michael let out a heavy breath and turned to Wheston. "And what the hell is astral projection?"

"It's a form a meditation, like an out-of-body experience."

Michael glared at him. "Meditation? Isn't meditation a form of relaxation?"

"Yes."

Michael glanced at Tess before returning his glare to the FBI agent. "Does she look relaxed to you?"

Jake and Agent Black were parked a short distance away, and she watched them climb out of their car and walk toward them.

Jake was the first to draw close. "Is something wrong?"

"Yes," Michael said, his voice raw with emotion. "Tess needs something to drink more than the water Agent Wheston brought. Jake, can you go inside and get her something sweet like soda or tea with lots of sugar?"

"Dr. Adams—" Agent Wheston began.

Michael cut him off by holding up his index finger. "She looks like she's in shock."

"Shock? What happened to her?" Jake demanded, and Agent Black echoed that question.

Michael took them both in while Tess took one deep breath after another. "Lean forward," he instructed her. "Put your head between your knees. Breathe in through your nose, out through your mouth, nice and even." He looked up at Jake. "She had another *episode,* as he so casually likes to call them. Jake, could you please go get something for her? I'm serious when I say I think she's going into shock."

Jake hurried off, and Markus Black stuffed his hands in his front pants pockets and frowned at her.

"I think I'll be okay." Tess sat up, taking measured breaths as Michael had instructed.

"Yeah, and except for the fact that you look pasty, you look okay." Michael refused to take his hand off her shoulder.

"No, really, I feel better now."

Michael reached out gently and turned her face toward his as he studied her closely.

"What?" she asked.

"Red marks that look like fingers on your cheek, Tess. What the hell happened to you?" Michael asked, his voice so filled with worry, his throat felt tight.

"Perhaps Tess could tell us what happened from the beginning." Agent Wheston already had out his notebook.

Michael clenched his free fist and forced himself to remain still to keep from punching Wheston in the face. "I know this is important. I want to find these women just as much as you do. But can you please put a lid on it for just a few minutes, Wheston? Can't you see what this is doing to her?"

"Yes, I see it. I also see that there are five women whose lives may very well depend on what Tess can tell us."

For a long moment no one spoke.

"Can we just go home?" Tess finally murmured.

Michael thought her voice sounded so small, so fragile, so much like she did when he opened his front door the day before and found her standing there looking terrified.

She looked up at Agent Wheston. "I'll tell you everything, but not here. I want to go back to Michael's house. I feel safe there." She looked around, as if expecting the killer to suddenly appear in front of her.

For another long moment, Michael was almost positive Wheston would refuse her request, and Michael knew that when he did, he really would have to punch him.

But the man surprised him by saying, "All right."

Jake came rushing back, carrying a large plastic cup with a lid and a straw. He handed it to Tess. "Clear soda."

Michael couldn't help noticing the way Tess's hand shook as she took it, and he was glad to see her take a long swallow without having to be coaxed. He looked at Jake. "Thanks. We're heading back to my place now."

"I'll be right behind you."

Michael stood and looked down at Tess. "Are you all right to go?"

"Yes." She shifted so she could set the soda in the cup holder between the seats and grabbed her seat belt.

After she fastened it, Michael gave her shoulder another squeeze and finally released her long enough to move around to the driver's side and climb in.

He started the car, and after she lifted the soda, he took her hand.

"Don't let me go, Michael," she whispered.

"I won't."

"Can you at least tell me—" Agent Wheston stated from the backseat.

"Save it, or get out now!" Michael warned.

Agent Wheston didn't say another word all the way to Michael's house, but Michael noticed in the rearview mirror that he continued to stare at Tess.

Michael parked outside the garage when they arrived at his house. Small drops of rain sprinkled the windshield. He held Tess close beside him and together they moved to the front door, leaving the others on their own. He was glad to see some color had returned to her cheeks. To his horror, the finger marks had deepened and looked as if they might bruise. What the hell had happened to her, he wondered? How could this killer physically hurt her if he wasn't even present? If he could strike her face, could he also stab her with his knife?

Tess still held the large cup, and she took another drink as he unlocked the front door to let them all in.

He led her inside and to his sofa. "Here, lie down."

She was still pale and felt incredibly weak against him. He understood her need to help, especially when she felt responsible for the killer taking Madelyn Prange, but this was taking its toll on her. When she was reclined on his large sofa, and he sat down beside her. He refused to let go of her hand, wasn't sure if he could have released it if he wanted to.

"Do you feel up to answering some questions?" Wheston asked after several minutes passed.

Agent Wheston was so eager to ask his questions Michael thought he might leap out of his clothes at any moment. He looked down at Tess and considered making the agent wait longer until Tess had rested. But he knew Tess. She wanted to help these women, even at the sake of her own health.

"I guess," Tess said.

Michael still held her hand tightly, but turned his attention to Jake. "Jake, why don't you order some pizza? I think we could all use something to eat."

"That sounds like a great idea." Jake headed toward the phone.

"What would you like on your pizza, Tess?" Michael asked. He knew Wheston wanted quick answers, and he knew Tess wanted to give them. But if he could slow down the pace just a little, perhaps it would be enough to give Tess a rest.

"I don't know if pizza is a good idea," she said.

"How do you feel?" Michael asked. He wished he could look into eyes and see a way to help her.

"The soda cools my insides, which feel like they're on fire. That's why I'm not so sure it's a good idea to eat anything. In fact, my stomach couldn't be rolling more if I were on a boat in the middle of a storm."

"I've probably got something to give you for your stomach," Michael said. He reached for the throw that draped the sofa and covered her with it.

"Thanks anyway, but I think just giving it time to settle is best."

Michael gave her a nod and took a deep breath. "Are you

sure you're up to telling us what happened?"

It was her turn to nod, and the smile she offered him was small but genuine.

When the pizza arrived a short time later, the men had no trouble devouring it. Tess's single piece grew cold on her plate.

Markus Black sat down in a chair on the far side of the room by the cold fireplace and ate quietly. Agent Wheston started to ask his questions between bites, and if Tess didn't know better, she would have thought she was in the middle of an interrogation…

Michael slowly ate a piece of pizza, continuously reminding her of her untouched food. But it wasn't food she needed. It was Michael's touch, so simple, so genuine, and so warm. It kept her grounded. It gave her strength while she answered every question Wheston asked.

The first question was about the killer and where she was with him and ironically didn't even come from Wheston who had thus far been chomping at the bit. "Did you get any sense of direction that could tell us where the killer is or where he's going?" Markus Black asked in a quiet voice.

Tess didn't look at him as she replied. "Not really. The highway was two-lane, fairly empty but for one car I saw. There was a Marla's Diner. I've never seen that anywhere close by here."

Jake said, "That shouldn't be too hard to find. Now if you'd had said there was a QT or a 7-Eleven, that might not have helped much. Do you have a phone book, Michael?"

"In the kitchen, in a drawer under the phone."

Jake headed toward the kitchen. He came back and sat down in a chair across from Michael and Tess.

"These women did something to him," Tess stated thoughtfully.

"Like what?" Michael felt her tremble and held her closer.

"I don't know. He said that he'd release Madelyn Prange because she was innocent, but he insisted the others aren't innocent and deserve to be punished."

"There is nothing that links them together," Markus Black stated.

Tess looked at him squarely for the first time, and Michael sat close enough he felt her heartbeat speed up.

"I'm telling you, there is."

Markus Black licked his lips and got out of the chair. "Tess, we've checked every possibility. We've talked to families. We've checked school histories. We haven't found one single thing that links them together."

"Well, something definitely linked them to him."

Markus obviously decided to move on, because he cleared his throat and asked, "Can you give us a better description of him?"

"Yes."

"While you're doing that, I'm going to go get some ice for your face." Michael said, letting go of her hand for the first time.

"My face?"

With her fingers, she traced the marks on her cheek.

"It looks like he hit you," Michael said.

"He did. Twice."

Michael swore and wasn't certain who he'd like to hit first—Jake for pulling her into this investigation, Markus Black for whatever he might have done to her in past, or Agent Wheston who seemed so eager to question her about her abilities that Michael wouldn't be surprised to learn he planned to write a book about her. When it came right down it, he supposed he wanted to hit the killer most for hurting her.

"Will you be okay if I leave you alone for a few minutes?" Michael asked softly.

"Yes. I'll be fine."

He headed for the kitchen and Tess took the last drink of her soda. It's coolness felt much better in her stomach than the little bit of pizza she'd forced down.

"No Marla's Diner in this phone book. Do you have a computer with Internet access, Michael?" Jake yelled toward the kitchen.

"You can use the computer in here," Michael called back.

Jake looked at Tess. "Do you need anything?"

"I'll be fine. You don't have to worry about me, Jake."

He slowly stood up, stalling for time. "I know, but in all the time you've worked with me, I've never seen anything like this."

"Me, either," she said, trying to lighten the mood. "But if this is how I can help you find this guy, then I can do it."

He gave her slight nod. "Okay." He passed Michael at the doorway as he headed into the kitchen.

A short time later, he rushed into Michael's living room. "Not only did I find a Marla's Diner—west of here near a place called Lake Jackson, but a 9-1-1 call to the local PD came through a short time ago. It seems a woman claiming to be a victim of a kidnapping got dropped off there."

Chapter Eight

Things started happening fast, so fast, in fact, that Tess thought her head or the room or perhaps both, were spinning as both Markus Black and Jake got on the phone.

Agent Wheston stepped closer and knelt before her. "Can you concentrate on Marla's Diner? Do you think you can project yourself there?"

"I would if I could, but I don't know how." Her lack of ability left her as frustrated as he appeared. She didn't add that she didn't think she had the strength to try.

Michael said nothing, but reached down easily and grasped her hand.

The moment Markus Black hung up his phone, he said, "There are agents on the way to the Lake Jackson area and the State Patrol has been notified."

"I've got my people contacting the local authorities to find out about the area," Jake added.

"I hate to burst your bubble, but what if he's only passing through on his way to somewhere else?" Michael sat down on the sofa, closer to Tess. "Or if Tess spooked him, he may be driving with no specific destination in mind."

"So far, Tess has been right on everything, and at least now we've got a direction to look," Markus Black said. Then his phone beeped and he flipped it open. "Yeah? You've got something already?" He listened. Then he looked at Tess. "I'll be damned," he let out with a breath. "I'll be there as soon as I can get there." The phone flipped closed with a snap.

"What is it?" Jake asked.

Markus still stared at Tess. "The woman has been positively identified as Madelyn Prange, who made her way to Marla's Diner, after her kidnapper dropped her off on some back road in the middle of nowhere."

Tess's heart hammered in her chest. "She's all right?"

"She appears to have some bumps and bruises, skin abrasions where her hands were bound, but she's alive and at the hospital, under police protection."

"You're going there?" Jake asked.

"Yes."

Tess gave a mental thank you, feeling as if a huge burden was lifted from her shoulders. Madelyn Prange was kidnapped because she'd been mistaken for Tess. If anything had happened to her, leaving those three kids without a mother, Tess would have never forgiven herself.

"There's already a team on the way to the diner, and I've got a helicopter waiting." Agent Black told Wheston as he put on his coat. "I'll head up there and take a look around, and I'll call if there are any new leads".

Tess wanted to suggest that Agent Wheston go, too, so she could have some time to recover some of her strength. She was afraid, however, that if she did, he'd suggest she also go to see what she felt at the area where Madelyn was released. She knew she didn't have the strength for any more "episodes" with the killer right now.

Her thoughts were interrupted when Markus Black left and Jake glanced at his watch, saying, "I need to check in with my people and take care of some things, too. Will you guys be all right if I leave for a while?"

"Sure," Michael replied.

Agent Wheston looked at Tess. "Is there anything else you can tell me about your experiences?" When Tess shook her head, he asked, "What can you tell me about the astral projection itself? I know you said you don't know how you did it, but tell me what you felt. Did you see any flashing lights? Or did you have a headache afterwards?"

Tess fought the uncanny urge to giggle at the way he asked questions about things she would never have even thought of. In the end, she merely let out a deep breath and answered his questions as best she could. "I have no idea how I did it—I wasn't trying to. And I did have a terrible headache, but it was before. It was why I closed my eyes." She went on to explain everything she felt and didn't feel—like how she couldn't feel the motion of the van but she was able to feel him slap her. Agent Wheston wrote in his notebook. When she finished and assured him she had no further answers, he said, "I'm going to go touch base with my colleagues, too, see if there's anything we can come up with that will help you control this ability of yours so you can get more information."

"Have you ever seen anyone with my ability?" Tess asked.

Agent Wheston cleared his throat before he said, "No, but then every individual is unique, so their abilities are different and unique, too. It's a bit like handwriting. We all learn to make an A or a G the same way, yet everyone's handwriting is different even though we can usually read it. At the same time, we all grip the pencil a bit differently, too, even though the outcome of making a letter or a mark is the same. I just want to learn how you're gripping your pencil, so I can help you learn to hone your skill and use it to the best of your ability."

"And how do you plan to do that?"

"I'll just check out some things on our computer and talk to some colleagues, and I'll be back," Agent Wheston promised. "If you have any more . . ."

"Episodes or think of any more clues," Tess finished for him, then added, "I'll be sure to call you."

"Thank you," he replied.

Tess looked at him evenly. "We all just want to find these women alive."

Then Agent Wheston and Jake were out the door, too, and the house was suddenly as still as a tomb.

"Gee, it's like the aftermath of a tornado," Tess said.

"You can say that again." Michael eyed her closely. "How do you feel?"

"Better, not as weak. Those episodes or whatever they are drain all of my energy, but oddly enough, they don't make me sleepy. I just feel frazzled and antsy as hell, like I'm overtired."

Michael smiled sympathetically. "And I guess the inquisition that follows doesn't help, either."

"No, not much." Tess absently scratched her head. "I just wish I knew how to control it. For all these years, my gift—ability—talent—whatever you want to call it has been nothing more than visions and only when I take some dead person's hand. Now there's so much feeling. And when I was in the van and in his house, my senses were so heightened, so strong."

Michael sat down on the sofa next to her. "It was always more than just visions, Tess."

"What do you mean?" she asked, staring at him in confusion.

"You've never seen how you look or how you react when you take hold of a dead person's hand. When I watch you, I see so many emotions on your face. I think you live it, just like the victim does—with every emotion and feeling that goes with it—but until now you've always been able to control your reaction to what you see."

Tess considered his words, then said, "You may be right. When I was a little girl and touched my grandmother and saw my uncle with the pillow, I was hysterical when I came out of the vision. Maybe I did just learn to control my reactions after that."

He put an arm around her shoulder, and Tess took a deep breath and snuggled close to him. His clean, blue aura was like a soft electrical current buzzing through her and recharging her. "I'm really glad he let Madelyn Prange go."

"Me, too."

"I couldn't say anything when Markus Black told us. I was too afraid it wasn't true and the bubble might burst."

"I know. I felt the same way too. You did it, Tess. You convinced him to let her go." Michael kept his answers short. He wanted her to let everything out. He wanted her to know he was there for her, no matter what. She was quickly turning to him, taking his hand and not being skittish about his closeness, so the last thing he wanted to do was push her in any way and lose the ground he'd gained.

"You heard what I said to Markus Black, didn't you?"

"About not having to touch dead people in order to see things? Yes."

"Did you hear what I said about being number fifty-two?"

"No." He decided to jump in with both feet. "What are you talking about? Fifty-two? Is that like Area fifth-one, or something?" He attempted to lighten the conversation with some humor." Before she could reply, he jumped ahead. "You

don't have to talk about any of this if you don't want to."
Although he wanted nothing more than for her to talk about it.
He wanted her to share everything with him.

She grinned at his joke then turned serious.

Michael saw the debate in her eyes on whether or not to
continue.

She continued. "We worked a case, kind of."

"Kind of?"

"I don't know if you remember it. It was four years ago, a
girl killed by a hit and run. There was thought perhaps she'd
been a victim of a kidnapping, so the FBI was here
investigating," she explained.

He shrugged. "I don't remember," he said absently.

"It's not important. It was the first time I met Markus. He
was nice. He took me to the movies. We saw some funny,
stupid movie, one of those chick flicks where the girl wants a
boyfriend with a lasting relationship and the guy just wants in
her pants."

Typical, Michael thought. Isn't that how it always worked?
Hell, he'd like to be in her pants right now. He swallowed and
waited for her to go on.

"Before that, he treated me to a nice dinner. Over all, it
was a nice date. I spent most of my growing up years being
shunned or called a freak, so I didn't have many dates."

Immaturity at its best, Michael thought dryly but kept to
himself to allow her to keep talking.

Afterwards, we went to this quaint little coffee shop that
had just opened up. There were lots of people there, people
who talked to me because they didn't know about my 'gift' or
my past, people who talked to me because I was with a good
looking guy. I felt so normal. It was wonderful. What was
even more wonderful was that my so-called 'gift' didn't kick
in when I touched him, which made me feel really normal. He
was really into these small touches. He held my hand or put his
hand on my back as he allowed me to walk through a door
ahead of him, and he put his arm around me during the movie.
I know that sounds like no big deal, but touch has always been
a major thing for me, you know?"

"Yes, I know." He absently ran his fingertips along the top of her thigh. Touching her was a major thing for him, too.

"I must have been like some deprived kid with a bag of candy just gobbling it up as fast as I could. We had coffee and shared a single piece of pie with two spoons." She stopped for a moment.

Michael allowed her to catch her breath.

"He asked me to come back to his hotel room, and I did."

She looked down as if she couldn't meet Michael's gaze. He took his hand off her thigh. With his fingertips, he gently forced her to look at him. He hoped she saw understanding in his eyes. "Go on."

"He kissed me."

The room was quiet for a long moment.

"And?" Michael asked.

"And I saw so much, so many flashes, like pages of a book that you flip through quickly. Girl after girl after girl, as well as the idea of a competition between Markus Black and a high school friend. And I was pegged as number fifty-two. It made me so sick to my stomach, to see how he treated women, how little respect he had for the gender. He went to the bathroom, and I left. I reached the lobby before I threw up all the coffee and pie. I was sick not for myself but for all the girls who didn't have a clue as to how he'd used them."

Michael met her gaze and held her closer. His action speaking louder than any words.

She smiled at him, a small knowing smile. "You know the really ironic thing?"

Michael was afraid to ask. And yet, he wanted nothing more than to stay where he was and hold her. Nothing felt as right as when she leaned her head on his shoulder and molded herself against him. "What?" he asked.

"He never truly believed I had any 'gift' or could see anything until today, until I told him the number he'd pegged me to be. And it felt good to tell him what I did. It was like closure, I guess."

Her hand was now on his thigh, and Michael liked the feel of it. It sent tiny sparks of warmth into him, and they all shot upward.

"And do you know what else?"

"I can hardly guess." He didn't care what else as long as she never took her hand off him. It would be better though if it was skin to skin without the material of his pants between.

"He touched me today and I think this case has changed him or at least bothered him. I didn't see any flashes of girls, only worry and something that edged along fear."

"Well, that's good."

"Yeah, I thought so, too."

The room was silent for along moment as he relished in the feel of her. The only sounds were that of their breathing, their hearts beating and the sounds of rain on the roof.

"Tess?"

"Yes?"

"Will you do something for me—honestly?" His heart beat faster.

"Yes, what?"

"Tell me exactly what you see when *I* do *this*."

Chapter Nine

When he brought his lips to hers, Tess shivered in Michael's arms. Her response caused his heart to quicken as he deepened the kiss. She smelled of exotic flowers with a hint of vanilla, and she tasted delicious.

Warm and soft in his arms, she seemed to melt against him. With all the emotions that bombarded her with touch, he knew it might be easier for her to be alone. He wasn't sure he could break through the walls she'd put up around herself, but he was willing to give it his best shot. Because no matter what she felt from touch, he wanted to touch her. He wanted to be with her.

He paused his kiss long enough to whisper, "Can you trust me, Tess? I won't hurt you." He emphasized his words by cupping her soft face in the palms of his hands.

"Your touch feels so good, so right. I can't turn my back on that. I want to trust you," she said softly.

That was all the encouragement he needed, and he leaned close and kissed her again. Softly, sensually, she kissed him back.

He pulled away from her lips and kissed a trail from her mouth to her neck.

More softness…

More sensuality…

Her subtle woman scent was intoxicating. The feel of her pulse beating in her throat sent his heart racing in unison with hers, and heat pulsed through him. He pulled her closer, and with a deep, throaty moan, she arched against him.

Michael didn't remember moving, yet his hands were suddenly under her t-shirt. Her breasts filled his hands. Her warmth moved through him like a river of lava. His palms and fingertips felt highly sensitive as they traced the exquisite stitches of the lace on her bra. Through that lace, he felt her nipples.

He was forced to back away from kissing her neck when

she moved to raise her shirt over her head. Her bra was blue, pretty, and brilliant against the subtle glow of her pale skin, and its color nearly matched the blue of her eyes.

Slowly, she unbuttoned the buttons on his shirt. Once she had it open, she tentatively touched him. Michael thought she touched him as if she'd never touched human skin before, as if she had to study the texture of it, the softness or hardness of it, as if she needed to examine every contour and crevice.

The slow, light brush of her fingertips was a great deal like rubbing two sticks together. Inside him, a fire started with a small spark, but quickly heated up. He forced in a breath, and the expansion of his lungs pushed his chest farther into her palms. She started and nearly pulled away from him.

"No, don't stop," he let out. "I love when you touch me. And I doubt there's anything you can say to get me to stop touching you."

"It does feel . . ."

"Wonderful?" he suggested with a smile.

"Yes." Her words were breathy, and her breaths were gasps.

"Exquisite?"

"Yes."

"Perfect?"

"Yes."

"Intense?"

"Definitely."

He kissed her again. He thought his heart might try to beat its way out of his chest with the way she teased his tongue with hers. He'd kissed a few women since he'd lost his wife, and he couldn't remember any of them turning him on like this with a simple kiss. Not that her kiss was simple. In fact, it was far from it. It was as if it sent a raging river of need and want and desire coursing through him.

Her pretty, blue bra hooked in front, and he easily unhooked it. When she didn't protest or move away, he eagerly put his hands on her.

Skin touching skin.

Heat against heat.

He couldn't believe it was finally happening. Michael felt like a virgin teenager—hot, needy, enthusiastic and filled with wanting. At the same time, the emotions that rocked him with her touch, with her very closeness, were deeper than a bottomless pit. His desire and his *need* swirled through him and melted into his core, where the heat from them threatened to burn him.

It was true he'd wanted her before, wondered about her before, thought about her, yet he'd never known until now just how much he wanted her, needed her. She was suddenly like his other half, the part of him that kept him alive. He also knew that after today, he would simply want and need her more.

Her breasts filled his hands with softness and fullness. Her ribs, her flat abdomen, and the curve of her waist that snaked to her hips were so soft he could have been touching silk, and he couldn't touch her enough. Like a man dying of thirst who suddenly finds an oasis, he couldn't drink in enough of her. He kissed her neck again before he moved lower. She tasted of honey, sweet and clean and pure.

At the touch of his lips to her breast, her moan cut through the room's stillness and was music to his ears. She tilted her head back, giving him greater access to her body.

"You're beautiful," he told her softly, terrified that words might break the spell they shared, yet needing to tell her how he felt.

She pressed her palm against his chest. "I feel your heart."

Before he could respond, she suddenly slipped out of his grasp and stood. Michael's hands ached with the loss. He was about to beg, to plead, for her not to be afraid of him, not to leave him when he needed her.

He stopped when he saw she'd stood to unbutton her jeans. With her blue gaze locked with his, she slowly slid the jeans down her legs. He grinned when he saw she wore a purple woman's version of men's briefs.

She stopped, a smile twitching at her lips. "You aren't laughing at me, are you?"

"Never. I just never would have believed anyone could make something that looks like men's briefs look so sexy."

She giggled, but Michael heard a slight hesitancy in her laugh. He knew he had to reassure her, so he took her hands and pulled her close again, murmuring, "Come back here, I'm not through kissing you. And if you read my mind when you touch me, then you'll know that I want only to bring you pleasure."

She smiled and kissed him fully on the lips. "I plan to do more than just read your mind."

Michael shivered as she unfastened the button of his jeans.

Chapter Ten

Michael held Tess close as the afternoon blended toward evening. "It sounds like the rain has stopped," he said. As if in reply, the windows rattled from the wind while thunder rumbled in the distance.

Tess sighed against his chest.

"Take a shower with me." Michael leaned over and hotly whispered the invitation in Tess's ear. He felt a shimmer move through her, and he followed it with a brush of his hand over her hip. Making love with her was like taking a walk on the sun—bright, hot, exhilarating and beautiful.

"There's definitely enough room for both of us in there," he assured her as he moved her hair out of the way and kissed her neck. "So what are we waiting for?"

"I like lying here against you." She snuggled closer.

Again, he moved his hand down the length of her. "I know how you are about touch, how it affects you. Imagine it with slippery soap suds and hot water and steam."

"Mmmm. That's quite a fantasy . . ."

"Well, are you ready to take it from imagination to reality?"

"What if I can't handle it?" She sounded half serious.

"If it gets too intense, I'll stop." It was a promise he hoped he would not have to keep because he wasn't certain he could stop once he again held her in his arms.

She apparently trusted him, however, because she climbed out of bed, and he followed. Moments later, they were warmed by streams of hot water and rising mist. There was plenty of room in his shower, but they stood face-to-face, his body pressed against hers.

He slid his hands over each side of her waist and down her hips, leaving sudsy bubbles in the wake. "Can you handle this?" he murmured, his words warmer than the water in her ear.

Tess shivered against him. It wasn't a shiver from the cold, but from the heat. "Maybe," she whispered. Then she smiled slowly.

"I like that slow, do-it-some-more smile," he said.

"I like the way you touch me, and yes, please do it some more." She leaned closer to him. The sensation of Michael's hands sliding over her skin really was almost too much to endure. Her every nerve quivered and jumped like a hot wire. The trembling that moved through her over and over sent her heart racing.

Yes, it was nearly too much to endure, but she didn't ask him to stop. In fact, if he stopped right then, Tess thought she might die. Her nipples were hard and peaked, a reaction that seemed to turn Michael on, too. He moved his palms over her entire body, yet he continued to return to her breasts. The water was hot, the spray hitting them from all sides. Michael's mouth was even hotter as his lips covered hers and his caresses moved lower, dipping between her legs. She moaned.

"Too intense?" he asked, jerking his head up and regarding her uncertainly. Tess couldn't help noticing how rough and husky his voice sounded.

"No," she forced out. "Intense, but not too intense."

Before, they'd engaged in a slow, gentle exploration with tentative, experimental moves. Not this time. This time was all heat, lust, and burn. Need driven by endless need. And the water of the shower did nothing to put out the fire they created.

Michael dipped his fingers into Tess's warm wetness, while she filled his blood with fire. The softness of her skin, intensified by the soap, seemed to call out for his touch. She arched against him, enticing him with her invitation. Michael tasted the sweet flesh of her throat she offered. A gentle nip of her teeth on his shoulder, followed by the hot brush of her tongue, nearly caused him to snap in two like a twig.

He shuddered, fighting for control, and she laughed softly. The sound of her laughter was deep and throaty and erotic.

"I always knew you were a woman of many mysteries. And I plan to investigate every one of them," he told her.

As he spoke, she cradled his face in her hands and forced him closer so she could kiss him. She tasted of willing woman. For a woman who claimed to have had so few kisses, she sure knew how to heat him up with one. He thought if she made him much hotter, the shower's spray would begin to boil.

When she slid her soapy hands over his chest, then down his sides, he gruffly said, "I'm glad you're not afraid of me, not afraid to touch me."

Tess looked up at him, her gaze both soft and tempting. "I don't think I could be afraid of you," she confessed. "Not now. I stopped being afraid after the first time you touched me."

He slid his hands down her back. "I wish we hadn't waited so long."

"For what?"

"To feel each other's touch."

She drew his head back down to hers, and they were quiet for a long moment as their mouths met for a long kiss.

Then she moved her lips to his ear and whispered, "Does it bother you that I see so much when you touch me?"

He raised his head and smiled down at her. "As long as it doesn't bother you that I see so much of you." Then he kissed her again as he sat down on the stone bench and watched the spray rinse the soap from her breasts. Then he leaned forward and put his mouth where the soap had been a moment before. Tess groaned and shivered, as Michael drew her nipple into his mouth. Then he eased her down so she straddled his hips. His essence filled her so completely, she cried out with the pleasure of it. Being on top, with Michael able to move very little filled Tess with a sense of power and control she'd never experienced before.

She met his gaze, and he asked, "Do you like this?"

"Definitely."

"Tell me what you're thinking."

She offered him a small smile. "I think I really like it this way."

"I like the way you feel this way, too."

"It's more than that."

"How is it more"

"I have little control over so many things—what I feel when I touch things. But this, doing it this way gives me control, puts me in charge."

He grinned at her. "Yes, it does. Please, Tess, take charge of me." With his hands on either side of her hips, he helped her.

The entire experience was more erotic than anything Tess could have dreamed—from making love, to washing one another, to drying one another. He couldn't seem to touch her enough, and Tess loved touching him, exploring him, learning his body and feeling his goodness surge through her with every touch.

When they returned to the bedroom and she reached for her clothes, he stopped her. Without a word, he slid his shirt up her arms and buttoned it starting with button just below her breasts, leaving a great deal of cleavage exposed.

"I knew it would look better on you than it does on me," he murmured huskily.

Tess couldn't have stopped her smile if she wanted to, and she didn't want to. But would this last once the killer was caught? She didn't know, but she decided to grasp every moment she had with Michael so she'd have those memories to hold onto if everything ended.

* * * *

An hour later, they sat together on the living room floor on a blanket in front of the fireplace. A tray covered with tea boxes and mugs of hot tea nearby.

"It isn't quite a picnic in the park, but it will do in a pinch," Michael said.

"This is wonderful," Tess replied. She still wore only Michael's shirt, but she had rolled up the sleeves, and she relished in the feeling of the soft cotton brushing against her bare backside. Michael's clean, enticing outdoors scent touched her everywhere the shirt did. And beyond where his shirt touched her, his skin touched her as they sat close enough for their knees to touch. Even that simple touch sent quivers into her legs. She studied Michael, who wore a simple pair of plaid flannel pants and nothing more. "Yes, this is better than the park. We couldn't be half naked in the park like this, at least not without people staring."

Tess giggled.

"Or without us getting arrested, especially when I couldn't keep my hands off you."

"Watch this," he told her as he picked up a nearby remote and pressed a button. Fire sprang up in the fireplace. "Instant bonfire."

"Wow, that was fast. You didn't have to use a flint or rub two sticks together or even flick your lighter," she teased.

"And convenient. I doubt I burned a single calorie lighting that gas log."

Tess chuckled. "It's perfect."

They scooted a bit closer to the flames, yet still sat close enough to keep their knees touching. It was as if neither could stand the idea of any space being between them.

Michael lifted a small white box of Chinese take-out from the floor beside him and handed it to her before lifting the other for himself. The food had been delivered a short time before, and when she opened the box and the food's aroma hit her, she suddenly realized she was ravenous..

"So what's your favorite color?" Michael asked as he began to eat. Unlike her, he didn't bother with chopsticks. He merely dug into his beef lo mein with a fork. "I bet it's purple."

She shrugged. "You're close. It's either blue or purple, depending on my mood. I'd guess your favorite color is green."

He grinned at her. "What makes you say that?"

"Your bathroom towels are green."

"So?"

"So is your car."

"Coincidence."

It was Tess's turn to grin as she caught a bite of broccoli beef with her chopsticks. "So are your kitchen towels, as well as your kitchen counter."

"Okay, so I guess that's too much of a coincidence. But I didn't really pick out the counter. It was here when I bought the house. And I couldn't very well get blue towels, they would clash."

"Definitely."

"I guess green might be my favorite color." Michael was quiet for a long moment as each of them took a few bites.

Then he put his box on the floor and carefully took her hand in both of his, sandwiching her fingers between his. Slowly he said, "Actually, the towels were a wedding present." He couldn't help noticing that his words stopped Tess mid-bite.

"You're married?"

"*Was* married," he corrected.

At least she continued to chew. "Divorced?"

"She died."

She looked stricken. "I'm so sorry."

He shrugged, not really knowing what else to do. "Hell, I wish I had a quarter for every time I've heard those words. I could quit my day job."

When Tess stared at him and said nothing, he said, "I'm sorry, Tess. I shouldn't have said that. I know you were sincere."

Tess glanced down at her food and Michael didn't like that she looked away from him. He could read her emotions so much easier when she met his gaze. Now he couldn't begin to guess what she thought. Then he was relieved when she took a small bite. At least she didn't appear to have any plan to put down her Chinese food and leave.

"Do you want to talk about your wife?"

He heard the hesitation in her voice. "I think the question is, do *you* want to talk about my wife after we just made love in my shower?"

"I don't know. I know she isn't here, but is she someone who can still stand in the way when it comes to us?"

It was a moment before Michael could reply, as if he had to look around for his wife or think about the question. "No, she isn't."

"Okay. Was it an accident?"

"No. She had breast cancer."

"Oh, Michael, I am so sorry," Tess said.

When she placed her hand on his arm, he looked up at her and saw the sadness and sympathy in the depths of her eyes. "So was I," he said. "We'd only been married a few months when we discovered the lump. I was still in medical school, trying my damnedest to be a great husband and a good student, and working toward being a great doctor."

For a moment, he lost himself to the past, remembering. When he pulled himself back to the present, there was only a slight hissing sound from the gas log in the fireplace.

He glanced over at Tess. "The lump was just the tip of the iceberg. The cancer had already metastasized to some of her organs and into her bones. The doctors couldn't save her. The chemo couldn't save her. And as much as I loved her, I couldn't save her."

Tess stared at him, her eyes bright with unshed tears. "It wasn't your fault, Michael. It was a disease. And I'm sure she knew you loved her so much that you'd have done anything to save her."

Her statement caught him off guard. "Oh, yeah, she knew how much I loved her. But in the end, does that make any difference?"

She looked down into her take-out box. "It would to me." Then she looked up and took a deep breath. "This isn't her . . .I mean we didn't . . . well, in her bed . . "

"No, Tess. That wasn't her bed nor is any of this her furniture," he said, gesturing around the room. "After she was gone, I spent a few months living in limbo. I couldn't even begin to tell you what I did or where I went—I simply don't remember. Then suddenly, it was as if I woke from a nightmare. It was seven months after her funeral, and I was sitting at an outdoor café, with a cold cup of coffee in front of me, and I felt alive again. Like maybe the clouds had disappeared and the sun came out. Sounds funny, doesn't it?"

When Tess merely shrugged and took another bite, he continued, "It was like I suddenly knew right then that it was time to move on with my life. I'm not saying I had climbed into the grave with her, and I'm not saying I moved on quickly, but I did leave the limbo. I finished school, but changed my specialty to pathology, and I moved out of the apartment we'd shared and got rid of almost everything. Most of the furniture was hand-me-downs anyway, and I felt like the reminders that came with all the other stuff did nothing but eat at me. When I landed my job, I bought this place, and my two sisters helped me decorate it."

Tess smiled. "You did a great job."

"Well, it is home. We even had Thanksgiving dinner here last year."

"Wow, I know you make a mean breakfast, but that's impressive."

He smiled. "I had a lot of help. And I didn't make the turkey or the dressing."

"What did you make?"

"The pies." He took a bite of food, deciding that he loved conversing with her. He loved it almost as much as making love with her. And in a way, it almost felt as if they were making love with words. Even though the topic of their earlier conversation had been grim, it was now easy and light, full of exploration and discovery as they got to know each other.

"What are you smiling about?" she suddenly asked, eying him suspiciously.

"I was just thinking how easy it is to talk to you. After I lost Emma, I didn't think I'd ever find anyone who made me feel as . . . whole as she did, so I never really let myself get attached to anyone. Then this mysterious, pretty woman with hair the color of honey and the bluest eyes I've ever seen walked into my cooler, and I guess I've been waiting for her to notice me ever since."

He noticed she licked her lips before she asked, "And what happens now that she's, um, noticed you?"

"I want to keep getting to know her," Michael replied without hesitation. "I want learn more than her favorite color and her favorite food. I guess I want to see just how far the mystery goes. And I'd be lying if I said making love with her once was enough."

Her expression grew serious. "I have to take this slow, Michael. My ability—"

"Doesn't bother me in the least," he interrupted quickly. "I know it takes your time and your energy—it's like a job for you. I know it's unpredictable and what you're dealing with right now is probably terrifying. I know it is for me. But it's not going to scare me away, Tess. I want to be right here holding your hand through all of it."

She suddenly looked very small sitting next to him, and her eyes looked huge as she held his gaze. "Thank you. It is scary. But it's not so bad when I'm not alone."

"Good." He took a bite of his food. "You said something about a lack of control when we were in the shower."

For a long moment, Tess didn't meet his gaze. She stared at the fire for long moment. "Most people don't understand what it's like to never have control over what happens to them. I can't control when or even if my visions will come or how long they'll last. I don't even have control over whether or not my vision will help or if it will just add confusion to the mix."

"I think I understand what you're saying. It's like not being able to control when it will snow. Or like when you lose control with an orgasm?" he added with a teasing grin.

He'd wanted his words to soften the mood, and obviously he'd succeeded because Tess chuckled. "Yes, I guess. But it's so frustrating when it doesn't happen."

"Like an orgasm?"

"Yes, I guess," she said with a laugh. "Except for the part where Jake Williams is standing there watching me, waiting for information to help solve the crime."

"I can see where that might make things uncomfortable. I sure wouldn't want Jake standing over me while I was trying to have an orgasm."

Tess laughed. "You shouldn't have said that. Now every time I have a vision, I'll probably be distracted by the thought of an orgasm."

"Is that so bad?"

"I don't know yet.

"Are you up to that game of gin rummy?"

She grinned. "I'll probably whip the pants off you."

He waggled his eyebrows at her. "Now there's an idea I like. Maybe I'll let you do just that."

She set down her food. "Why don't we just skip the game and let me whip the pants off you. We could call it strip poker without the poker."

"I think the poker will definitely be there . . ."

Laughing they fell into each others arms, while not far away, a murderer—with his thoughts centered on Tess—used his knife on his next victim.

Chapter Eleven

Tess stared at the fire. She and Michael lay on the floor with the throw from the sofa covering them. With the fire in front of her and a sleeping Michael pressed against her back, she felt toasty, fulfilled and content. In fact it was incredibly hard for her to believe there could be anything wrong in the world, much less a murderer who would probably love to sink his knife into her.

How could she have shied away from Michael's touch for so long? How could she have ever been afraid of him? She recalled the story of his wife. He'd said that after she'd died he'd lived in limbo. Well, Tess knew exactly what limbo was. She'd lived there most of her life, hiding from people, from their emotions and from their touch. With a smile, she snuggled closer to Michael. Because of him, she would never have to reside in limbo again.

But as she watched the gas log's flickering firelight, reality began to creep back in. She tried not to think about the remaining women the killer held captive, and she hoped Madelyn Prange had given the authorities some helpful clues to help them catch this monster. Hopefully, Jake, Markus Black and Agent Wheston already had that information, were hot on the man's trail, and they just hadn't had time to call to let her and Michael know.

Even as she gave herself that pep talk, a sense of foreboding overtook her. She tried to shake it off. After all, the killer had dropped Madelyn Prange off several miles west of here, and by now he was probably hours away, probably even in another state.

And even if he wasn't that far away, he couldn't know where she was because they hadn't "connected" since she'd been at Michael's house. And if he could somehow figure out where she was, he'd never get past the cops outside. She was with Michael who, she knew, would do everything within his power to protect her. She should feel safe.

So why didn't she?

She closed her eyes and tried to relax. For a moment, she thought her breathing and her heartbeat mimicked Michael's, and then . . .

. . . her heart slammed against the wall of her chest when she opened her eyes to find the gas log cold in the fireplace. Her back was cold, too, because Michael no longer touched her. Slowly, she turned to find he still slept, although he'd rolled onto his back and now lay several inches away. Tess shivered against the sudden coldness that raked at her like sharp claws. The house was quiet as a tomb and just as cold. For a long moment, she was frozen with terror.

Then, feeling a strange sense of weightlessness, Tess rose to her feet. With fingers that felt thick and slow, she buttoned up Michael's shirt. It did little to fend off the cold that continued to claw at her.

"Michael?"

He didn't appear to hear her and continued to sleep peacefully.

Tess, however, felt far from peaceful. Her scalp prickled. Her chest was tight, making breathing nearly impossible. Time after time, she fought down a bone-clattering shiver.

"Michael!" she screamed.

When Michael still didn't move, she knew she was having another vision, but she had no idea what to do. Except this wasn't just another vision. She could feel the killer's presence, but that didn't make sense. The past two times she'd connected with him, she'd projected herself to where he was, so why was she still in Michael's living room?

The answer touched her with icy talons of terror.

The killer had to be here, too. Inside Michael's house.

No, that couldn't be possible. She'd already determined that he couldn't possibly know where she was, and even if he did, he couldn't get past the police outside. Besides, he had to know the police were looking for him, so why would he risk coming back?

She turned slowly to look at the clock on the mantle. It was nearly ten. It had been more than eight hours since they'd gotten the call regarding Madelyn Prange. The killer had had plenty of time to turn around and drive back to the windy city.

But if that was true, it still didn't explain how he'd found her.

Confused, she looked down at Michael's sleeping form, and the answer slammed into her. When Michael was touching her he kept her grounded, but he'd rolled away from her in his sleep. Without Michael touching her, had the killer been able to somehow connect with her?

Painful, terrified heartbeats counted out the seconds as Tess did nothing but stand frozen in place and listen. She felt as if she floated, and her senses, at least hearing and touch, seemed to be heightened immensely. If the killer was here, she should hear his footsteps or smell his odious locker room scent.

"Michael?" she tried again, although this time she spoke softly, urgently.

Michael sighed and rolled farther away from her. As he did, some inner instinct made her look up.

The killer stood in the doorway, complete with greasy hair. He still wore the same jeans and sweatshirt over a faded green t-shirt.

Tess stared at him, unable to breathe. Unable to move. He couldn't be here. *He couldn't!*

Then he grinned at her, a slow, cold grin that left her feeling as if she needed a shower.

"I knew I'd find you," he drawled. "It just took me longer than I thought it would."

Tess glanced down at Michael and mentally called to him, trying to wake him.

"Don't bother trying to wake him up. He's out for the count. It's how we meet like this, you know. I finally figured it out. We're not awake. All of us are sleeping."

Tess gave a sharp shake of her head. "That's not true. You were driving when I was in your van."

He chuckled bitterly. "Yeah, I was driving all right, had been all night thanks to you for making it impossible for me to stay in my house. The next thing I know you're in the van with me, and then I suddenly wake up on the side of the highway and you're gone. It was probably a good thing you came along when you did. I'd apparently fallen asleep at the wheel, and I might have had an awful, maybe even fatal, accident. So thanks for saving me."

He was thanking her? she thought in disbelief.

"Are you working with the cops on this, trying to find me?" he asked.

"Yes. And they will find you." She'd obviously scared him enough before that he'd released Madelyn Prange, and she tried to scare him now by putting some force behind her words.

He gave a negligent shrug. "I don't doubt that they will. But will they find me in time to save the other four women? That's the part that's doubtful."

"Where are they?" she asked, again adding force to her words.

He smirked. "Like I'd tell you."

"Where are they?" she persisted.

"Are you this pushy with him?" He nodded toward Michael. "If you are, I don't see why he keeps you around. Even if you do have hot legs."

As he gave her legs a slow, lascivious look, she fought against the urge to fall to the floor and weep, giving him what little advantage she held over him. She drew in a deep breath and said scathingly, "Go to hell."

"I've already been there—spent an entire month there— in a deep sleep, as a matter of fact. Since I woke up, I've had to live every day without the only girl I've ever truly loved, thanks to the women in my van and the others I've already punished. So if you think you're going to convince me to let any of them go, you can forget it. They deserve everything they're going to get from me."

Concentrate, Tess told herself. *Concentrate on moving back into something resembling dreamland so you can wake up.* It was the only way she could think of to get out of this nightmare.

Suddenly, he scowled at her. "Stop it! You're trying to leave. I can feel it."

She'd like to scratch out his eyes and see if he could feel that. "If you aren't going to tell me anything helpful, I see no reason to stay any longer—or to allow you to stay here. In fact, I find you boring, so why don't you get out?" She tried to keep her voice flat, tried to sound like she was bored. She let out a huffed breath to emphasize her words.

"Boring?" He grinned again and Tess shivered. "I'm far from boring, as my lady friends can tell you. By the way, I managed to find your house for real. I'm so sorry about getting you confused with that pretty lady from Oak Park. But to make up for it, I left a present for you on your porch."

Present? She didn't even want to contemplate what kind of present he would leave on her porch. She doubted it was a bouquet of flowers or a box of chocolates.

Tess fought against another shiver, closed her eyes and shook her head, hoping to clear the terror she felt, hoping, wanting, *needing,* to get rid of him.

When she opened her eyes again, she jerked awake.

The fire still burned in the fireplace. She was still on the floor, and as in her dream, Michael slept on his back behind her, a few inches of space separating them.

With a gasp, Tess jerked into a sitting position, trembling all over, feeling as if she were freezing and burning up at the same time.

Michael awoke instantly. He sat up, his expression filled with concern. "Tess, what is it?"

"He was in here!" She jumped to her feet, but when she tried to stand, she was too weak and nearly fell.

Michael was beside her instantly, and he managed to catch her before she landed on the floor. "Hey, hold on." He glanced around. "There's no one here. You must have been dreaming."

"No," she insisted. "It was more than a dream. It's how I've been connecting with him. It happens when we're both asleep. Or at least when he's asleep since I don't think I was asleep at the gas station. I think I only have to be relaxed. But he was here, standing in that doorway," she said, pointing toward it. "I spoke to him, and . . ."

Again, she looked toward the doorway where the killer had stood, almost expecting to see him standing there, but it was empty.

Yet, the cold essence of his evil lingered in the room, and Tess couldn't help shivering. "Oh , Michael. We have to get to my house. I think he's left something terrible on my front porch."

Chapter Twelve

Tess had doubted the killer would leave her flowers, and yet, as she stared up at her own front porch from the front seat of Michael's car, she saw that was exactly what he'd left.

The flowers were beautiful. Roses, carnations, and lilies caught in wisps of snowy baby's breath, and whimsical greenery all tied together with a brilliant pink ribbon. They seemed the capture the filtered light from the streetlight on the corner and hauntingly reflect it out into the night's darkness.

"Stay here. Don't get out of the car until Jake gets here." Michael grasped her arm, as if he didn't trust her, when she put her hand on the door handle. "He's going to be mad enough that you came here to see what this guy left on your porch."

"The cops he assigned to guard us escorted us here and they're right there," she pointed out, as if Michael didn't notice their flashing red and glue lights or the way the fog cast the colored light in odd directions.

"They only agreed to escort us when you refused to ride in their car and threatened to come by yourself."

"Michael, it's my house. I have every right to see this." She let go of the argument, pointing out something else to change the subject. "Look, there's a card. I can see it from here. Gosh, that's the biggest vase of flowers I've ever seen."

Three seconds later, Jake arrived in his own car. He actually double-parked next to Michael, so his car was in the street. He climbed out and Tess watched him. First, he talked to the two uniformed officers who had escorted her and Michael. Then he and the two cops quickly scouted the area. Jake had his gun drawn. Tess couldn't see if the others did, too, but she was certain they did. When it appeared there was no danger lurking in the mist, Jake approached Michael's window.

"It looks like he's already gone, and I've got an investigation van on the way to dust for prints and check for any other evidence.

The fog grew soupier by the minute, but Jake's sudden

anger was clearly evident despite it. "And you did the right thing by calling me and explaining everything, but you should have never come, Michael. What were you thinking, bringing her here?"

Michael started to reply, but Tess beat him to the punch. "I told him either he could bring me or I'd come by myself. My car is, after all, parked in his garage."

"And I thought my bringing her was better than letting her come alone," Michael added.

"Geez, you two are a piece of work," Jake muttered as he pulled out his cell phone. When he hung up from calling for help, he said, "Tess, can I have the key to your house? We'll need to look inside in order to investigate thoroughly."

She reached across Michael and handed her keys to Jake.

Within minutes, her house was invaded by a team of FBI agents, which included Markus Black and Agent Wheston, as well as a crime scene van.

Jake gave her keys to Agent Wheston but still refused to let them get out of the car, much less go near the porch or the strangely beautiful vase of flowers. "Take her home, Michael—to your house."

"We can't go there," Tess insisted. "It's no longer safe. He knows about Michael, and he can find us there. I'm still not sure what he sees when he looks at me, but I sense that he may now know what I look like."

Jake let out a long, frustrated breath. "Fine, I think you should be in police custody for protection anyway."

"I can't do that, Jake. This guy seems to be able to read my thoughts when he connects with me. If we go to a hotel or motel, he'll be able to find me easier. If I stay at police headquarters, he may learn whatever I see or hear and he'll know where you are in your investigation. If I'm going to get any sleep, I have to do it at a place that isn't even familiar to me so that when he probes my thoughts, I can't tell him where to find me."

Michael took her hand. "So how do we do that, Tess, by blindfolding you?"

Tess knew that what she'd just said sounded ridiculous,

but she had no other clue as to how he'd found her at Michael's. She knew she hadn't intentionally connected with him and told him where she was. She also knew that Michael was only trying to find the best way to help the situation.

She met his gaze. "Maybe you should blindfold me," she said slowly. She had to force herself to look away from him as she watched the FBI agents go through her front door.

She swallowed hard at the lump in her throat and held Michael's hand so tightly, she was afraid she might break his fingers, despite the fact he said nothing and didn't pull away. She forced in a deep breath as tears filled her eyes at the sense of invasion, the loss of control, the fear, terror—the ultimate assault on top of previous assaults. Her insides churned the Chinese food she'd eaten earlier, and when she thought she couldn't handle any more, she looked back at Michael. In his gaze, there was warmth and a sense of safety. She clung to that as if it were a life ring.

Jake drew her attention by saying, "I'll take you somewhere else for the rest of the night. You'll like it. But first, Agent Wheston and Agent Black need to ask you a few questions."

She let out another heavy breath. "All right."

"I know how these visions leave you exhausted, Tess. But maybe you know more than you think you know and you'll be able to give them a clue as to where this guy is. Wheston's pretty mad that you left Michael's house and came here. He said something about the killer may have left vibes there and that he would have rather questioned you there where the feelings might be stronger. But he'll settle for asking his questions here in the car."

She met Jake's gaze. "I couldn't stay at Michael's after he'd been in Michael's house," she whispered. It was impossible to explain the cold evil that she felt from the killer. Michael's house was warm and safe, and the killer had found a way to breach that. She couldn't let it happen again. So now she had to stay away until this monster was caught.

"Okay," Jake said.

She and Michael watched Jake move up her front steps and into her house.

"Do you think we could just leave now—sneak away and disappear into the fog?" she asked, only half joking.

"I think Wheston would hunt us down with as much enthusiasm as he's using to track down the killer."

"Yeah, that's what I was afraid of." Tess looked out the windshield at the fog and tried to relax, while at the same time she tried to gear up for Agent Wheston's questions. Michael, still holding her hand in his, brought it up to his lips and kissed it. Tess said nothing, but she couldn't help wondering what he saw when he looked at her. He said her ability didn't bother him, but she knew this couldn't be easy for him to watch. And now it had to be even harder knowing the killer had been in his house, had invaded his personal space—had been close enough to see Michael sleeping—all because the man was after Tess.

Tess was sure Michael wasn't very happy about that, and as she looked up at her own house she understood. The killer had been here, and this would never again feel like home.

She felt Michael squeeze her hand, and she gave him a small smile before looking back toward the fog. Right now they were tied in this together. But how would Michael feel once this was all over? She nearly laughed as a line from a song popped into her head: Would he love her tomorrow? Unfortunately, it was an appropriate question. Would she appeal to Michael as much when the excitement of this case was over? Would she even look the same to him when there was no danger?

Then the questions were lost in the fog as Agent Wheston opened the car's back door and climbed in. He waited to start the inquisition until Agent Markus Black climbed in on the other side.

Once they were settled on the backseat, Tess turned in her seat so she could see them. Over the next several minutes, they made her repeat her conversation with the killer word for word three times. By the time she finished, her mouth was dry and her insides felt as if they shook.

She couldn't decide if she was angry or simply exhausted when Markus Black said, "There is absolutely nothing that connects these women. You have to be wrong about that."

Tess's temper flared. "I don't care if you can't find a connection between them. To him, they are all responsible for the loss of someone he loved. And remember, he said he'd been in hell—in a deep sleep." She paused and thought about that, then she looked at the older man. "Agent Wheston, you asked me if I'd ever been in a coma. I haven't, but I think he has. I think it's how he's able to connect with me." She paused again, and frowned. "I also think that every time we connect, he gets better at it. The first few times I went to him. This time, he was able to come to me." She looked at Michael. "It makes me afraid to relax."

Michael gave her a reassuring smile. He still held her hand and his felt like the only grounding force in the world. Markus Black had flipped open his phone and was dialing. Agent Wheston was writing in his notebook. Tess knew that what she'd given them were small leads, but they were leads.

While Agent Black gave low commands into his phone, Agent Wheston looked up from his notebook and said, "Detective Williams says he knows of a safe place for you to go for the night. Agent Black and I will take this information back and see if we can find anything that will help us catch this guy. We'll be in touch."

With that, he opened the door and climbed out. Agent Black quickly followed.

Tess expelled a heavy, loud breath once they were gone.

"Are you okay?" Michael asked, his tone concerned.

"Oh, I'm just dandy. I can't sleep or relax without a killer popping into my head. My house has been invaded about three times now. I don't think I'll ever feel safe again, and I have no idea how to control this new ability. At least with the regular visions, I can control them by not touching a dead person." Then she met his gaze through the darkness of the car. "I'm sorry, Michael. I shouldn't be ranting at you. You've been nothing but supportive through all of this."

"Forget it."

Although his words were innocuous, Tess heard impatience in his voice. He still held her hand and she felt a tension in him that flowed from his hand into hers.

Before she could ask what was wrong, he said, "What's happening here, Tess?" Now worry, concern, and anxiety mixed in with the impatience in his voice.

She had a pretty good idea what he meant, but she still asked, "What do you mean?"

Michael cleared his throat. "I mean that ever since we made love in front of the fire, you've gone back to putting up a wall between us. I thought we were past this, so why are you doing it now?"

It wasn't after they made love, she mentally corrected. It was after the killer showed up in his doorway, but she didn't correct him. Nor did she tell him the wall was to keep him safe, that she thought it best to distance herself from him in case her new ability got dangerously out of control—not that she had any control over it.

For a long moment, the car was eerily still. Tess didn't think either of them even breathed. Finally, she couldn't stand the silence any longer. "There's no wall," she lied.

He let out a huff that was nearly a sarcastic chuckle. "Right. You're sitting here with me, holding my hand, and at the same time, you might as well be a hundred miles away."

And even with Michael holding her hand, she had never before felt so lost or isolated. She closed her eyes for a brief moment and rubbed her face with her free hand. "What the hell do you expect?" she let out, her words little more than breathy whispers.

"I expect you to trust me."

She looked right at him and stared into his eyes, eyes she'd rather get lost in right now than deal with this conversation. "I do trust you. It's this monster, this killer, I don't trust. And he wants to kill me—at least I'm pretty sure that's what he'll try to do if he ever really gets his hands on me. I don't want you close to that."

"I think I'm old enough to make my own decisions on what I want to be close to and what I don't."

His voice was even and controlled. It was in his hand she felt the subtle twinge of anger, as if he tried to hide it from her. It reminded Tess of a pot of simmering water—the kind that could suddenly boil over if it wasn't watched closely.

"I understand that," Tess said since she didn't know what else to say. She couldn't let him be in danger because of her, she simply couldn't. She cared about him too much. She might even be in love and . . .

No, she refused to go there right now. She couldn't think about anything so personal, so emotional, so life changing as love, not when there was a maniac after her.

"Do you?" he asked.

For a moment, Tess couldn't remember the last thing either of them had said, so she took a moment to run their conversation over in her head until his question made sense. "Yes, I do understand. And do you understand how this is for me? How frightening? How terrifying?"

He let out what sounded like another sarcastic chuckle. "Probably better than anyone else. Why can't you understand that you don't have to deal with any of this alone?"

"I've never been anything but alone—especially when it comes to this."

Michael squeezed her hand and brought it closer to him. "But you're not alone anymore."

Tess was saved from having to address that comment when Jake's knuckle tapped on the window and startled them both.

Tess took in a deep breath and forced her pounding heart to slow as she reached for the window control.

"Agent Black says it's all right for us to leave, and he or Wheston will call me if they find anything in your house, Tess— or if any new leads come up." Jake glanced at the house as he spoke. "Although if they find out anything new, it will probably be from the information you gave them. Given what little evidence this man has left in the past, they're probably wasting their time here." Jake rose and stared at her house.

Tess didn't say anything nor did she follow his gaze. She knew that if she did, the sight of all those dark suits would haunt her dreams, just as the killer did. Instead, she looked at Michael. He still held her hand tightly in his.

"You can follow me," Jake called out as he moved away from them and toward his car.

"Will do," Michael replied loudly before Tess raised the window to close out the fog.

"When we follow Jake, I want to lie down in the seat. I don't want to see where we go. If the killer is able to read my mind, I don't want him to be able to figure out where we are."

"There's a lever on the side of the seat that makes it recline almost to the point where you're lying flat. Use that, then you can still wear your seatbelt and hold my hand," Michael said.

"Okay, but you have to keep talking to me, keep me awake and alert. I'm scared to death to even do more than blink or relax. Knowing my luck, and my inability to control this . . . this . . . whatever it is, I'm liable to connect with him and bring him right into the car with us."

Michael offered her a lopsided grin. "You don't have to worry about that. I'll keep you talking. I don't want him in the backseat any more than I want Agent Wheston back there."

Despite the stressful situation, Tess couldn't help chuckling. She found the lever and reclined the seat back. Michael looked over at her. "Comfy?" he asked.

"You bet," she replied, forcing her voice to be light. Then she laughed softly.

"What's so funny?" he asked, starting the car.

"It's not funny as much as black humor. I just had this horrible thought."

He looked over at her through the darkness. "More horrible than what we've already dealt with?"

"Yes. What if I reach the point where I have to keep driving around in order to avoid this killer?"

Michael let out a heavy sigh. "Then I guess we'll learn where all the cheapest gas stations are."

"That's one thing I like about you, Michael. Your perspective."

He grinned at her. Then he turned serious. "Are you leaning back far enough? Can you see out at all?"

"I'm not looking out," she assured him. "I'm either looking at the ceiling or at you."

"Good. Here we go." He put the car in gear, but before he pulled away, he again took her hand.

"I bet you're tired of listening to me talk," she said after a while. They'd only been driving for about fifteen minutes, but it seemed much longer to Tess.

He glanced over at her and then back up at the road. "Nope."

"Liar."

"When are you finally going to get it through your thick skull that I'm here for you, that you aren't in this alone?"

Even though she heard frustration in his voice, Michael let go of her hand and gently fingered her hair with one hand as he drove. His touch distracted her. His scent distracted her.

"Tell me more about your brother," he said. "What's his name again?"

"Tom.""

"Right. Tom. So, tell me a story about him. Something you remember him doing when you were kids."

"Okay. Once he and Eddie Fortman and some other boys from our neighborhood were playing marbles. Marbles were a big deal when my brother was about nine or ten. Well, my brother won this beautiful blue marble from Eddie, but Eddie refused to let Tom keep it, despite how everyone said Tom won it fair and square. My mother told Tom he had to give it back. But instead of giving it back, Tom put it in his mouth and swallowed it."

Michael laughed, and Tess smiled at the memory.

Michael glanced over at her again before he turned the wheel and they obviously went around a corner.

Tess closed her eyes and tried to clear her mind so she wouldn't think about what direction they were going.

"Did it ever come out?" Michael asked.

Tess smiled again. "Eventually, but Eddie Fortman didn't want it back after that. Now that I think about it, my brother didn't play with him very often after that, either."

"It was probably a good thing. I'd hate to think what more your brother might have had to swallow if he did." He made another turn, this time to the left, and finally stopped. He looked down at her. "We're here."

"I don't want to look. I don't want to see anything that

might give up a location."

"Do you really want me to blindfold you and lead you inside?"

"No. I'll just keep my eyes closed." She ignored the slight dizziness that slid through her as she sat up with her eyes closed and listened to Michael climb out of the car. In her mind, she saw his actions, his every move, his fluid steps around the car.

Then he opened her door, and as he gently gripped her and began to guide her out of the car, the warmth of his hand on her arm was electrifying. It seemed without vision, her other senses were heightened to the point that they nearly overwhelmed her. She smelled moisture in the air even through the rain was over for now. The dampness sent coldness to her cheeks. In the distance, she heard two, perhaps three, dogs barking and the faint music of a radio, then a thud of a door slamming somewhere.

But stronger than everything, she felt the heat and familiarity of Michael's touch as he helped her to her feet and put his arm around her. Tess snuggled against him and let him guide her, doing her best not to be clumsy. She heard Jake's footsteps ahead of them.

"Up three steps," Michael instructed.

"Where do you get your patience?" she asked softly.

"I was number six of seven kids and grew up in a house with only one bathroom."

"Oh, my! I guess that would do it."

"Yeah, but my dad's pretty smart," Michael went on. "We only had one toilet and one tub, but he hung mirrors in nearly every room."

As he spoke, she remembered something he'd said yesterday, and she asked, "So when you said everyone came to your house for Thanksgiving, did they all come?"

"Yep, complete with spouses and kids, and my parents, of course."

"And your two sisters helped you decorate your house, so you must have four brothers?"

"Yep," he said again. "Up two more steps."

"We must be under the porch roof or an overhang. I don't

feel the mist in the air here."

"That's right, Jake's opening the door. Up another step."

She felt the sudden warmth of coming indoors, but she still didn't open her eyes until she heard the door close and a lock slide into place.

"You can open your eyes." She recognized Jake's rough, sandpapery, I-just-woke-up voice.

For a moment, the light hurt her eyes and Tess couldn't focus. When she could, she found herself in a foyer, looking directly at a photograph of Jake and a woman with dark hair. "Is this your house, Jake?"

"My humble home, yes."

"I don't think this is a good idea, Jake. If the killer connects with me, it could lead him here. Just like at Michael's house."

Jake looked at her. "But you don't where 'here' is, Tess. I know I'm taking a chance, but you knew how to get to Michael's. Your car's there. You'd driven there, right?"

"Yes, but—"

"But I'm banking on the idea that even if he connects with you and sees the inside my house, he's going to have to do a great deal of homework in order to find me. Even if he is able to find out my name, my phone number and address are unlisted. And just for the record, if he does manage to somehow make his way here, your next stop will be a very generic hotel room. Right now, however, I'm buying a little time."

"All right," she finally agreed, not liking the idea of involving Jake's family any more than she liked involving Michael. But she was too exhausted to go anywhere else just then.

So she looked around Jake's home. It was not what she'd expected. The floor was hardwood, the hall table long and narrow. On that table was the framed photo of Jake and the woman. The photograph that hung above it was large, showing the profile of that same beautiful woman with dark hair. Her wedding dress had an exceptionally long train.

Tess looked to the doorway that led into what appeared to be the living room and saw the woman with dark hair standing there staring back at her. At least Tess thought the woman in the doorway was the same woman as the one in the photograph.

They resembled one another, but the living one seemed smaller, older, with thinner hair and an innocence that didn't seem to fit her quite right.

"You're Tess," the woman said.

It wasn't a question, but Tess answered anyway. "Yes, I am."

"I would know you anywhere."

"You would?" Jake asked.

Emily smiled brilliantly. "Of course, I would. You know that, Jake. Don't be so silly."

Jake stared at her for a moment before he said, "Tess, Michael, this is Emily."

Tess looked up at the photograph again. "Is—"

"Let me take your jackets," Jake interrupted.

His smile was forced as he took Tess's jacket.

"Would you like to play chess with me, Tess?"

At the woman's question, Tess felt something off kilter, but couldn't quite put her finger on it. She looked at Jake.

"Do you mind playing a game with her?" he asked.

"Of course not. I used to play with my brother when we were younger."

"He moved up from marbles?" Michael teased as they all followed Emily into the living room.

"Yes, ended up qualifying for State in high school and placed third."

"Wow," Jake said.

Tess couldn't help noticing that Emily was oblivious to their conversation as she sat down on one side of a small table that held a chessboard and pieces. The pieces were scattered about the board, and Emily quickly put them in their rightful places. Slowly, Tess sat down across the table.

"I get to go first," Emily said. Without taking a breath or even a pause, she went on. "Jake, can we have some macaroni and cheese? Tess likes macaroni and cheese."

"I'll make some in a few minutes, Emily. First, I'm going to get Tess and Michael something to drink. I'll bring you a drink, too."

Emily moved one of her pawns, but when Tess moved to

do the same, Emily stopped her. "Wait, it's still my turn."

"Okay."

To Tess's amazement, Emily moved four times total before she looked up and said, "Now it's your turn."

Tess moved a pawn.

After a few seconds, Emily let out a heavy, impatient breath. "Are you going to take your turn or not?"

And Tess discovered she got to make five moves before it was Emily's turn again. "I think this could be a very interesting game, Emily," Tess said carefully.

"Every game is interesting, otherwise I wouldn't play."

Jake set a cup of hot chocolate in front of each of them.

"Thank you," Tess said.

"Can we have our macaroni and cheese?" Emily took a deep swallow of her chocolate.

"You have to wait. It's still cooking," Jake replied patiently.

Tess glanced under the table to see Emily swinging her feet beneath her chair as she moved several pieces. Her chess moves were made with little hesitation and what appeared to be little thought. But as Tess looked at the board, she realized they were more than random moves. Emily might not be taking the correct number of turns, but she still moved each piece as they were supposed to move—the knight two up and one over, the bishop diagonally, the rook in straight lines, and so on. And she was moving them to advance on Tess's king, as the game should be played. Furthermore, she moved each piece to block any move Tess would make.

Several minutes later, Jake placed a bowl of macaroni and cheese in front of Emily and another bowl in front of Tess.

Tess wasn't really hungry, but she didn't argue the issue. From across the room, she met Michael's gaze and noticed he held a bottle of beer but wasn't drinking as he watched Tess and Emily play.

"Michael, would you like some macaroni and cheese or can I get you something else?"

"Michael likes macaroni and cheese, too." Emily spoke without missing a beat in moving her queen to put Tess into check.

Jake looked at Michael and Michael shrugged. "I do like it, but I'm not sure how well it will mix with beer."

"Emily, Michael and I will just have some pretzels."

Emily ignored them as Tess moved her bishop to protect her king and put Emily's queen in jeopardy. Unexpectedly, Emily moved her queen out of harm's way and put Tess back in check with a rook.

Tess looked at Jake as he held up the bowl of pretzels as if silently offering her some. She shook her head and watched as he, also silently, motioned for Michael to sit on the chair before he sat on the sofa where he faced both her and Michael. He placed the bowl of pretzels on the coffee table. Absently, he turned on the television with the remote, but didn't turn to watch it.

"I can talk now," he said softly, but loud enough that Tess could hear him. "The television, the game, and the mac and cheese will be enough distraction for her that she won't listen to anything I say."

He leaned forward, placed his elbows on the coffee table, steepled his fingers and rested his chin on them. Tess thought he looked more exhausted than she felt.

During his pause, Tess took the opportunity to move her queen.

"I met Emily five years ago." He grinned at the memory. "I got shot, actually—just a flesh wound through my arm, but wounded in the line of duty. She was a nurse in the emergency room. She held my hand and calmed me down, and I think I fell instantly in love with her." Jake paused and looked at Emily.

She kept her gaze on the chessboard and took a spoonful of macaroni, clearly unaware that Jake was talking about her.

"We were married a year later. She comes from a big Italian family, and they accepted me as if I'd been a part of the family forever. It was the happiest day of my life. The next two years were like a dream, a wonderful dream. We lived and loved. We planned our future, bought this place, gutted it and rebuilt it with the help of her cousins."

He paused and grinned. "She has a cousin who's a contractor, a cousin who's an electrician, and a cousin who's a plumber, so we had all the bases covered." He paused and looked at Emily with something close to sadness in his eyes. It made Tess's heart ache.

"She loved me like no one's ever loved me, flaws and all. Then, one night, she decided to stop on her way home from work to pick up a dozen eggs to make my favorite cookies. She walked into a convenience store in the middle of a hold-up. I guess the door chimes spooked the guy, and he shot her."

He paused again as if he couldn't readily go on. Then he took a deep breath and licked his lips. Tess had to look beyond Michael to look at Jake, and she noticed that Michael never moved as he listened. He held the beer and never took a drink or never reached for a pretzel. The beer was probably warm in his hand, and for the life of her, Tess couldn't concentrate on the game, not that it was easy to think ahead three or four moves anyway.

"You can't move your bishop that way," Emily said suddenly when Tess made a move. "He can only go this way." She used a pointed finger to point in a diagonal direction on the squares.

"Oh, sorry," Tess said, looking back at Emily as she listened to Jake.

"The surgeons were able to stop the bleeding in her brain, but they couldn't remove the bullet without killing her. At least without killing her quickly. No, they thought it was better leave it there and let it slowly kill her while we all watch. So that's what it's doing, there inside her head. I went from having this loving, bubbly, fun, smart, adoring wife that I wanted to grow old with, that I wanted for the mother of my children, to suddenly having a child in a woman's body, a child who spends her days eating nothing but macaroni and cheese. She can't see logic in anything, can't tell time or even figure out the sequence to use the remote and turn on the television. She can sleep for an hour or for twelve. And she can spend hours randomly moving chess pieces around the board."

"I don't think her moves are random," Tess said.

"It's your turn," Emily said.

Tess put her spoon down to move.

Jake rubbed his eyes and chuckled bitterly. "Not random,

huh?"

"No. I think she anticipates my moves."

"Why do you think that?" Jake asked.

"I have your bishop," Emily said with a smile as she took Tess's bishop with her bishop in an unforeseen move.

"Because she's beating me. And even though she moves several moves at a time, it seems she does it because she's anticipating my moves," Tess explained staring at the board, amazed she could talk about Emily and not distract Emily from the game.

"Do you want to know the strangest thing?" Jake asked.

"What?" Tess said.

"I told her about you months ago. I don't remember when. It was during a case. But she's never forgotten you. She can't remember to put her socks on before her shoes. She can't remember our wedding day or even that I'm her husband. She can't even see she's the beautiful woman in the portrait, but she remembers you. She asks about you every day."

"Every day?" Tess asked in disbelief.

"It's still your turn," Emily said.

Tess obediently moved her knight to another spot, even though she'd already moved four other times in a row.

"You're making this easy for me, Tess," Emily said.

Tess smiled at Emily as she picked up her queen and took a bite of her food with her other hand.

"Yes, every day," Jake said. "And now she's having these episodes." Tess shot him an irritated look, and he said, "I'm sorry, Tess, I know how Wheston must make you feel using that word. But I can't think of a better description of what happens to Emily."

"What kind of episodes is she having?" Michael asked.

"She's zones out. You know how some people have epileptic seizures without shaking, like they just stop and stand there, like somebody hit the off switch in their brain?"

"Yes," Michael answered.

"It's like that. She can be in the middle of a sentence and suddenly stop. Then half a minute later, she continues where she left off. She can be in the middle of a bite of macaroni. She might have just lifted her king off the board. It doesn't matter. It's like time stops. She's perfectly still. She doesn't even blink." Again he paused and licked his lips. "And these zone-outs are becoming more frequent and last longer each time." He rubbed his eyes and leaned back on the sofa.

"Checkmate," Emily said.

Tess looked up and forced a smile at Emily. It was, indeed, checkmate.

Jake let out a couple of deep breaths and rubbed his eyes wearily. "It's time for bed, Emily."

"Can Tess sleep with me?" Emily stared at Tess with wide eyes filled with excitement and an equally wide smile. "We could have a flashlight under the covers and tell spooky stories."

Tess tried to hide her grimace with a smile. The last thing she needed was a spooky story since she was already living one. Oh, to live in Emily's worry-free world, Tess thought with a touch of envy that quickly dissipated.

"Some other night," Jake put in. "Go put on your nightgown."

At least she didn't pout like a child being sent to bed, Tess thought. She simply did whatever Jake asked her to do, as if she was programmed to do as he said.

Tess watched Emily move down the hall. Then she looked back at Michael. "I think I'll go wash my face." She picked up her small bag and followed Emily down the hall.

Michael watched Tess leave. "I wish I knew what to do for Tess," he said after she was gone.

"What do you mean?" Jake asked.

"I know she's afraid to sleep, or even close her eyes, afraid she'll connect with the killer—afraid she'll lead him to wherever she is, terrified she'll put someone else in danger. She talked all the way here so she wouldn't fall asleep." Michael paused and let out a bitter chuckle. "I'm caught between the idea of slipping her a sleeping pill to make her sleep or giving her a few energy drinks to keep her awake all night."

Jake met his gaze. "She doesn't connect with him every time she sleeps, though, right?"

"Right."

"I thought I heard her say your touching her keeps her grounded and keeps her from connecting with him.

"That's right," Michael replied.

"So stay close to her," Jake put in.

Michael looked at the sofa, remembering their first night at his house. "I plan to do just that. Do you have a few blankets?"

"The spare bedroom is all made up if you want to use it," Jake offered as he stood.

"I think we'll stay out here for a while, if that's all right if you," Michael said.

"Your choice. But I've got to get some sleep. I'm beat."

"Thanks a lot for helping us, Jake."

Jake met his gaze before he headed down the hall. "You're welcome. I'll be right back with some blankets."

Tess came back down the hall, her cheeks slightly flushed, as if she'd scrubbed them. Her flushed cheeks made her eyes appear a brighter blue. For a long moment, all Michael could do was stare at them. She had no idea how alluring she was. Her beauty was fresh and real and honest. There was no makeup shadowing her eyes or chiseling her cheeks and the finger marks left by the killer were fading. Michael fought the urge to cup her face in his hands and kiss her.

Emily returned, now wearing a long flannel nightgown. "Good night, Tess." Emily drew close and hugged Tess tightly.

"Thank you, Emily, and good night to you, too"

Emily drew away but still held Tess's hands. "And don't forget."

"Don't forget what?"

"If you put chocolate under your pillow, you'll have sweet dreams."

Jake, who came back down the hall with a couple of folded blankets, probably heard Emily's loud whisper, but he said nothing.

Tess held back a laugh, and smiled softly. "I won't forget."

Jake took Emily's hand and led her into the bedroom and closed the door, leaving Tess and Michael alone in the living room. Tess sat down on the sofa. Actually it was more like she dropped onto the sofa. "I wish it was that easy."

"Wish what was that easy?" Michael eased down beside her.

"Put chocolate under my pillow and have sweet dreams."

"Sounds more like you'd have a mess in the morning."

Tess let out a small laugh. "Yes, it does, doesn't it?"

Michael reached out and took her hand. "Tess, I know you're tired. You can rest here."

She met his gaze. "How do you know for sure?"

"Because we're going to sleep on the sofa, together, where there isn't room to roll away, where I'll be touching you every moment, so he can't find you." He let go of her hand so he could put his arm around her. Then he leaned over and took her with him so the two of them were reclining. "Kick off your shoes and relax with me."

"What if you're wrong? What if he comes here?"

"Then I'll still be here next to you, and we'll deal with him together." Hell, he hoped he was right. He hoped that idea was even possible. He was sick and tired of watching her be terrified and having no way to help her.

She leaned against him. He felt her tension as strongly as he felt her heartbeat, and her chest moved with each anxious breath.

"Relax." His word was hardly more than a whispered breath close to her ear. Her soft, vanilla, woman scent touched him, along with the softness of her hair as he leaned against her.

"It's not that easy," she whispered back.

"Sure it is. Just lean your head on me and relax."

She laughed bitterly.

"Tess, I know your past has taught you not to trust anyone, but you can trust me. I'm not going anywhere. You can lean on me and relax, and I promise when you wake up, I'll still be right here beside you." Michael didn't confess that he wanted to wake every morning next to her. Instead, he wrapped a tendril of her hair around his finger, unable to believe how soft it was.

"I've been thinking about him," she confessed after several

minutes passed.

She didn't have to tell Michael who "him" was, and he said, "Why would you want to spend your time thinking about him? He's nothing but a cold-blooded killer."

"I know, but I've been thinking about what it will be like when this is over, after he's caught and in prison where he belongs."

Michael didn't confess that he'd been thinking the same thing, but he'd been thinking more about where Tess would be. Still close to him? Still making love with him in front of the fire and under the spray in his shower? He certainly hoped so. "What about it?"

"I've been wondering if he'll still be able to connect with me. I mean, what if every night after we go to sleep, he leaves his cell and shows up in my bedroom?"

Michael bit his lip and didn't breathe for a long moment. It was the only way he could maintain control, and he had to remain calm. She was simply too perceptive. If he wasn't careful, she'd feel or see the way his insides had just shaken apart at her question. He had been too busy worrying about the present and hadn't even imagined the future.

"I know what you're thinking," she said softly.

Since he wished this killer would show up on a slab in his morgue, he doubted that. "Really, what?" he forced out, hoping she didn't hear the tightness in his voice.

"You're thinking about my ability and having second thoughts about us."

Michael looked down at her. "No, I'm not. I just told you, I'm here for you to lean on. And when I told you before I didn't care about your ability, I meant it. I still mean it."

"But that's what you meant when you were dealing with the old me. I can't control this new ability, and I'm sure it scares you."

"This killer scares me, and it bothers me to know that he scares you. But, Tess, you and your ability do not scare me. I wish I could make you believe that. Have you always been this stubborn?"

"Yes," she answered without hesitation.

"Ooooo, now that scares me," he teased. "Maybe I'll let you spend some time with my brother, Marty. He's only slightly more stubborn than you are."

Tess smiled against his chest.

Gently, he moved his hand up and down her back. "Get some rest. I'll be right here when you wake up."

"Okay."

A few moments later, he felt her relax and heard her breathing move into the slow, steady rhythm of sleep. He looked around and couldn't help feeling relieved to find no stranger in the room with them. Then he looked down and watched Tess sleep. He should be as exhausted as she was, but he was content to stay awake and watch her.

He didn't even realize he'd closed his eyes until he woke with a start at the sound of Emily's shrill voice yelling, "Wake up!"

Her hand was on his arm, tugging urgently at his sleeve to wake him.

And Tess was gone . . .

Chapter Thirteen

Raymond Bradford, the man who had quickly become Tess Fairmont's worst nightmare, looked around the dark cabin and sat down heavily. The bunk was old, musty and hard without the mattress that he remembered being on it years ago. He had his last three ladies tucked in, if he could call drugged and tied up tucked in. Soon, this would be over, and Mary could rest in peace. He nearly laughed at the thought since he was the one who needed the rest, especially after his little bout with Anna Carpelli. Yes, he'd lost a lot of blood and he'd had very little rest in the last twenty-four hours. He certainly needed it. He simply wasn't certain he wanted to take it. His kills always shot his adrenaline to the sky, and when it dropped back to normal, it left him feeling as if he could sleep for three days. He couldn't, however, afford to sleep that long.

He clenched his fists and worked to ignore what felt like hot oil in the pit of his stomach. He should have known better than to try something so daring as to bring them all here at once. It was much easier when he killed them one at a time, as he had with the first four. And yet, the idea of having a group of them on the bluff, just as they had been years before, had excited him as nothing else had. It just hadn't been as easy as he'd thought it would be.

And his most recent kill had seemed like such a waste, just mixing in with the past two. He hadn't wanted to kill Jill or Julie or Anna that way. He'd wanted them here. He'd wanted them to feel that rush of the earth coming toward them as they fell, even if he did get more excitement from using his knife. He told himself his latest kill should be no different, despite his ambivalent feelings for Anna Green, or Carpelli as she was now known. He had always liked Anna. She had been nice to him, pleasant even, and nice to Mary. He hadn't really wanted to hurt her. And it was those feelings, those memories that had caused him to let his guard down. He'd forgotten Anna was the most athletic of the group. Growing up, she'd played basketball and soccer. And now, as an adult, she was a well-accomplished climber, hiker and marathon runner.

So why had he forgotten and turned his back on her? Why had he given her the opportunity to beat the crap out of him and grab his knife and use it on him?

Because he was overtired. Because he'd thought the drug he'd given her would be enough to keep her docile and cooperative.

Still, there was no excuse, he scolded himself. She could have killed him. She could have ended it all, instead of royally messing up his plans.

In fact, he thought she may have hurt him really bad. She'd stuck him with his knife, right into his side, up to the hilt. And before he could even move, she'd managed to give the blade a good twist that sent an ocean of pain all the way from this toes to the top of his head. The pain and shock of it, mixed with his fatigue, had nearly driven him to his knees. His punch to her face had been nothing more than a lucky reaction. And after he pulled the knife from his own body, he hadn't hesitated to use it on her.

So instead of napping hours ago, as he'd planned, he'd had to get rid of her body. He should have gotten rid of it so the police couldn't find it, but he hoped that if he gave them another body, it would keep them busy for a while. That way he could accomplish what he'd set out to do so many months ago, even if there were only three of the women left. What a party that would have been, he thought, if they could have all again stood on top of that bluff together.

But that was not to be.

He reached back and touched the bandage on his right flank. It was wet and warm from the blood that oozed through it. Maybe if he could stop moving for a while, it would stop bleeding.

He tried to think of something that would help his wound. Hell, with all his medical "experience" he should be able to think of something more than the bandage he'd attempted to tie around his middle. But his thoughts seemed to be garbled. What would be done for him if he went to the Emergency

Room? He thought back to all the time he spent in the hospital. He remembered being poked and prodded all the time, but what did anyone actually *do* for him. He remembered he always had an IV. He couldn't get an IV now, wouldn't even know where or how to place one if he had the equipment, but he knew IV's kept the patient from becoming dehydrated. He should probably get a drink, he thought, to keep from becoming dehydrated from the blood loss. But he was too tired to get back up and get it. Instead, he lay down on the bunk and tried to close his eyes. He should sleep, but the pain that moved through him like waves wasn't going to allow it. He forced himself to his feet—slowly. Then he moved to grab his backpack. After a dose of over the counter pain reliever that would also help him sleep and several swallows of water, he let out a breath and forced himself to walk back to the cot.

He fell down on it. It would feel better in the morning, he vowed silently. He'd come too far to let go of the plan now. So what if there were only three left? They would be enough, and Mary would be at peace. He closed his eyes.

He tried to force every thought from his mind, especially thoughts of the woman who had invaded his dreams. The last thing he wanted was to have her invade them tonight. For some strange reason, meeting up with her always left him feeling more exhausted when he woke up than when he went to sleep. He knew he would have to deal with her eventually, just as he dealt with all the others. But right now, he was too tired.

His dreams were strange, as if he dreamed of being asleep and dreaming. In his dreams, he searched for Mary, but she was no where to be found.

Again and again, he continued to see the woman who haunted his dreams, the witch who refused to leave him alone. Yes, he'd have to get rid of her somehow, but later. Please, later. In his dreams, he walked through the campground.

There she was again—that witch.

"Leave me alone!" He thought he yelled, but only whispers left him.

Again, he saw her. This time, he didn't yell, he simply turned away, seeking darkness, seeking peace. He went farther into the woods, amazed his dream was so vivid he could smell the sweet, earthy smells of the trees. Mary should be here. She would love this.

He thought he saw Mary. He tried to run toward her. It wasn't Mary.

It was the witch. Again.

Fine, if she wanted a confrontation, he'd give her one.

* * * *

Tess waited several minutes after she was certain Michael was asleep before she moved. Carefully, she slipped away from him, having to slide to the floor before she stood and looked down at him. The house was dark and silent. Just as carefully, she covered him further with the blanket so he wouldn't feel cool wake.

She had no idea how long she stood staring down at him. Relaxed in sleep, his face was free of worry lines, his mouth slack. Tess licked her lips, thinking of how he had kissed her with those lips, how he had used them to taste her body, how they had seemed to leave a trail of fire on her flesh.

"I'm doing this for you." Her whisper was lost in the silence as soon as the words were out of her mouth. She had to do this. She had no choice. She could never be with him, could never have a free moment with him, if she didn't do this. If she didn't do this, the rest of her life would be spent always looking over her shoulder.

Without another sound, she picked up Michael's jacket and headed for the back door and out into the backyard where, if the killer managed to follow her, he could never see a street sign or a house number or even know the suburb where they were.

The early-spring night was black. There was no moon, and little light from the few stars that managed to peek through the fog. There was a street light close enough to cast eerie, filtered light into the backyard, enough that Tess saw her breath when she exhaled.

She sat down at the forgotten picnic table in the middle of the yard and fought down a shiver. She thought again of Michael, wanting nothing more than to be back inside, snuggled warmly in his arms—the only place she'd felt safe in a very long time. She forced a swallow through her tight throat, took a deep breath and closed her eyes.

Only then did she really allow herself to relax.

She had to know everything there was to know about this new ability. It was the only way she could learn to control it. And she couldn't do it with anyone else around. It would be too dangerous.

She closed her eyes and concentrated on the killer, on everything she remembered about him and took another deep breath. She pictured the killer's face in her mind. She brought forth the memory of his smell and had to swallow down the burn of bile.

Her senses heightened.

She heard a car go by on the street out front.

The dampness of the fog filled her nose and seemed to seep into every pore of her skin. There was even a taste of salt in the air.

Then the air grew dry again.

Slowly, cautiously, Tess opened her eyes. She still sat at a picnic table, but she was no longer in Jake's backyard. Her heart felt as if it might beat right out of her chest, and her mouth was suddenly as dry as a dessert. And when she attempted to lick her lips, it didn't help.

"Get a grip," she said softly. "You got this far. Now you can do the rest. You have to."

Her voice sounded hollow, but she recognized it, and it brought her some comfort.

She looked around. More stars twinkled down at her. The fog above was gone. Now there was only lingering fog that snaked about the ground. The scent of ashes and campfires from years gone by touched her and mixed with the slight fishy smell of a lake. Sounds of small critters in the woods drew her attention, but only for a moment. She didn't move as she took in all her surroundings—the nearby woods, the rippling movement of a lake down the hill from where she perched, the silhouette of what appeared to be a dark, unused cabin.

She had done it! She had been able to use this ability at her command. At least she thought she had. She wouldn't know until she saw where she was, and until she returned to where she'd started, she was only half done. But she couldn't think about that other half just yet.

Tess forced herself to stand up on legs that felt shaky, and took a deep breath to head off the lightheadedness that threatened her. Then, without a sound, she moved toward the dark cabin.

Moving was an odd sensation, as if she floated and her feet never touched the ground. Yet, her body moved as she commanded, although in seemingly slow motion. She continuously stared through the darkness, expecting the killer to come out at her at any moment.

The cabin had no glass in the windows, only screens. By the time Tess reached it, her eyes were well accustomed to the dark. She leaned close to the screen and peered into the deeper darkness. The smell of wood and dust and mold and blood touched her in an instant.

It was too dark to see into the cabin, but Tess heard the breathing of sleeping occupants. In fact, one of them actually snored loudly. The killer? She moved to the door and tried to grasp it, but couldn't.

Concentrate, she thought, concentrate . . .

Inside, she had to get inside. She had to see why she smelled blood. She had to see who was in there.

The door silently opened without her touching it. Tess floated into the ancient wooden structure. There was a rustic, musty smell in the air, but the small cabin held nothing but old platform bunks—four sets of them. One set on each wall.

And all four lower bunks were occupied with sleeping people. Tess, now accustomed to the dark and touched with a heightened sense of awareness, recognized the killer. She also recognized Olivia Brannigan and Shanna Brown and Sue Harper from her previous visions, as well as from their pictures that were posted at police headquarters. She saw the way he had them bound to the bunks. She saw the dark stain on the killer's shirt and jacket. Blood? It was too dark to tell.

What she needed to see was where they were, she decided.

This was obviously a campground or summer camp of some sort. Apparently, Raymond wasn't kidding when he said he planned to take them on a hike.

She moved back out the door and away from the cabin, looking up at the number posted above the door, but the number wasn't enough to tell her where she was. She had to find some kind of sign or something.

Which direction should she take? Away from the lake? Perhaps she should just look for a highway or some other landmark, or an office that might have paperwork complete with a name.

Tess felt herself take a breath. The night seemed darker, the night sounds louder, the air that entered her lungs colder. She moved up the hill away from the lake, but over the hill, she found only more trees, more forest.

She turned and walked in the opposite direction. Suddenly, she froze, tilting her head and listening. Had she heard someone moving in the cabin when she passed by? She tried to hurry away, to put some distance between the killer and herself, but she seemed to have little control over her speed. Whatever this ability was, it seemed to be either stop or go with nothing in between.

A short distance away, she saw more cabins and a path leading to them. She followed the path. It took her into the woods, amidst a strong smell of pine and moss.

After what seemed like hours, she was still in the woods. At a fork in the path, she took a left, only to come out on the edge of the lake. Across the lake, she saw the lit neon sign of a marina. She squinted, trying to read it. "The Happy Lender," she muttered out loud. "The Happy Lander . . ." She looked for something else, but nothing appeared familiar to her. She turned and went back. After another fork, she came out at a different place in the camp, seeing a different group of cabins.

She moved around them silently, becoming nothing more than a creature of the night. More fog settled in around her legs, now nearly up to her knees.

Instinctively, she looked toward the horizon, which was starting to lighten. Was it that close to sunrise? It didn't seem as if she'd been here that long, but then time seemed to move strangely in this dimension, seeming to speed by one moment and drag the next.

All of a sudden, the gray of early dawn touched her like cold fingers. It would soon be morning, and she still had no idea where she was. She needed the name of the campground where the killer held his intended victims. She couldn't be concerned about how time worked here. She had to be concerned with the fact that the killer would soon wake, and some inner instinct told her that when he did, the three women with him would soon be dead. She had to do more, had to find out where they were, but she couldn't move any faster.

With uneasiness mushrooming inside her, she tried to ignore the fact that she was getting tired. She tried to keep her breathing even, but it grew harsher and harsher. She would have to leave soon. If she didn't, she wasn't sure she'd have the energy to find her way back to Jake's backyard, especially since she wasn't really sure how to return there. Up until now, she'd had Michael to call her back, but this time, she'd have to find her way back on her own.

She moved around a bend in the path, expecting to find something new, hoping to find a highway or clubhouse with a name or a sign or anything.

What she found was Raymond standing in front of her.

Chapter Fourteen

"I thought I heard you. When are you going to leave me alone?" he demanded.

Tess wanted to run.

She tried to run.

She concentrated on the idea of running.

When it didn't work, she thought about merely putting distance between herself and him.

That worked, although slowly. If she didn't know better, she'd think she was backing away from him one step at a time. Then, as she watched him, she thought she really hadn't needed to worry about him. He seemed to fade in and out, becoming translucent like a ghost one moment before filling in with richer color the next. Tess was mesmerized by the sight. She could see the trees behind him—through him—then she couldn't. Yet, even with his loss of substance as he faded away, the color of frustration and anger stayed high in his cheeks.

"Dammit! I knew I shouldn't have taken anything for the pain so I could sleep! Now, I can't control this when I meet up with you!" He pulled out his knife, but it was as translucent as he was.

"What do you plan to do with them?" Tess worked to keep her voice even, to keep her expression and her words filled with authority. He couldn't know how terrified she was. He could never know that the only reason she was still before him was because she had no idea how to get away from him.

"I plan to take them hiking, just like we did fifteen years ago."

"What happened fifteen years ago when you went hiking?" she asked, hoping his anger would keep him talking.

To her frustration, he said nothing as he nearly vanished before her eyes. Several seconds later, he returned and stepped—no, he seemed to leap—toward her.

"Mary died." In his rage, it was apparent he screamed the words, but they sounded as if someone was quickly turning a volume knob up and down. "And I spent the next month living in a nightmare. And no one cared! Well, now they do. Now, these three care a lot! The others are dead, but by the time I killed them, they cared, too."

"How did Mary die?" Tess asked, frantically wondering how to get out of here. How did she get back to Michael? She tried to concentrate on Michael's face. She tried to think of Jake's backyard—the picnic table, the trees, and the wood fence—hopefully, none of those would give any hints to the killer.

When nothing happened, she decided that until she figured out how to return, she needed to get as much information as she could since the campground had given her no clues.

"She fell! She stepped on some loose rock, and her feet went out from under her. One second, she was standing next to me. I was even thinking about reaching out to see if she would let me hold her hand. The next moment, she was sliding away in the loose rock close to the edge of a cliff!" he finished waving toward the hills behind him.

Still in a rage, he looked as if his face might pop like an overblown balloon. Even in the darkness, his clenched fists were pale. "I tried to help her. I laid down to keep from falling and grabbed her hand. I told the doctors I couldn't remember anything, but I remember it all now, every slow second of it. I can still see her eyes, looking up at me, pleading with me, *begging me,* to help her. I had thought of nothing but holding her hand and then I was. But I couldn't hold on. I still feel the rough rocks scratch my arms as I tried to keep my grip on her, but I lost my hold on her. The edge was so close and the rocks were sliding away faster and there was nothing to hold on to. I can still hear her scream. Then I fell, too. I still remember that pull of the earth as it came crashing up toward me. Most of all, I feel the pain when I hit the rocks at the bottom of the drop. It felt like everything happened in slow motion and lasted a lifetime."

He let out a loud, huffed breath as he momentarily became transparent again. "And none of them cared enough to help either of us." Each word was stronger than the previous as he became more solid. "They just watched us slide down the rocks, and they did nothing to save us."

"What were they? Thirteen, fourteen, fifteen years old?"

"That doesn't matter!"

"Of course, it does. And how fast did it happen? Maybe they didn't know what to do or how to help. They were just kids, probably scared kids."

He shook his head furiously. "They didn't know what to do?" His mocking tone sent a shiver up her spine. "You think it happened too fast for them to help? That doesn't excuse them. Their lives went on as if nothing had changed. They didn't wear casts on their legs for months. They didn't have their vertebrae fused together. They didn't have to go to rehab to learn to walk again. They were able to run and play and participate in sports and march in the band without having to think about how to do it or take pain pills. And they weren't rotting in the ground like Mary. Well, now they all will be!"

"If she just fell, it wasn't their fault," Tess pointed out.

"Quit defending them. They deserve to die. I'm only sorry I couldn't push them all from the cliff at the same time. I'm only sorry I couldn't kill them all together, that only these last three get to experience the real thing. Although I did hit Richie Van der Moss with a rock several times before he died, so at least he got to feel the pain of rocks hitting him like Mary and I did."

Tess didn't know how she stayed on her feet. Fatigue gripped her and seemed to weaken every cell in her body. She had to get back to Michael, back to Jake's house, before she had no strength left. She closed her eyes and filled her thoughts with everything about Michael. She thought of how he made breakfast so enjoyable with sausage and bagels. She let the memory of his scent touch her. The thought of his lips on her filled her with much-needed warmth. She followed that idea with the memories of the warmth of his hands, his blue aura, and the earth-shattering feelings she experienced when he made love with her. Then she thought of Jake's backyard, the peeling paint of the picnic table, the night sounds, and the few stars that lit the yard.

She still heard the killer's voice, yet his words came to her as if from a distance as he yelled, "Wait! Don't go!"

When she opened her eyes, she was in Jake's backyard, her back to the picnic table as she stood about two feet from it, staring at the fence.

She had made it back. She had managed to escape Raymond.

Tess let out a long, heavy breath. She had left on her own, under her own control, and had made her way back alone, too. Of course it had taken quite a bit of concentration, so much, in fact, that she no longer had any strength left. She fell heavily to her knees and barely managed to keep from hitting her face on the fence's rough boards.

Tess shivered uncontrollably against the cold grass. With what little energy she had left, she tried to crawl toward the back door. She had to get to Michael. She needed the safety of his arms and the heat of his body. She had to tell Jake about the campground, about Raymond, about Mary. And worse, she had to tell him that now there were only three women left.

She barely managed five or six feet before she couldn't move any farther and collapsed. The last thing she was aware of was the cold grass against the side of her face.

* * * *

"Where's Tess?" Michael demanded, as he jumped off the sofa and nearly stumbled in his haste. He towered over Emily, but she stared up at him unafraid.

"She's . . ." She stopped and experienced one of the episodes Jake had told them about. She simply stared up at him, unmoving, unblinking. She didn't even breathe, Michael noticed.

"Oh, Emily, come back, come back." His words were only whispers, but the urgency in them caused his throat to grow tight. "Don't do this now. Please, Emily, snap out of it."

Seconds ticked by. With each one, Michael felt as if a small knife cut away another piece of his heart. He clenched his fists to keep from grabbing Emily's arms and shaking her until she woke from her trance and answered his question.

Michael glanced at his watch. How many seconds had

passed since Emily began her haunting stare? He had no idea. But one thing he did notice was that nearly six hours had slipped by since he and Tess had fallen asleep on Jake's sofa. How long ago did she go wherever she went? He turned away from Emily and hurried toward the front door to search for Tess.

"In the backyard." Emily voice stopped him in his tracks. He swung around to see that she was back just as suddenly as she'd gone, and she didn't appear to know that she'd even been gone.

"What's going on? Emily?" Bare-chested and barefooted, and wearing only a pair of jeans, Jake came down the hall toward them.

"Tess is gone," Michael said. "Emily says she's in the backyard." With each word, he raced toward the back door. He glanced back at Emily. "How long has she been out there, Emily?"

"Seventeen years."

Jake followed him, saying, "Emily has no concept of time or numbers, so you're wasting your time asking her how long Tess has been gone."

Michael pulled open the back door and scanned the backyard in the gray light of dawn. Then he saw her sprawled on the ground.

"Oh, Tess . . ." He raced down the steps and ran toward her, each step feeling too slow.

When he reached her, he dropped to his knees beside her. She was cold to his touch and limp when he carefully turned her onto her back. Her face was so pale he felt as if like ice water had been dumped over his heart. He quickly checked her over for broken bones, and when he didn't find any, he wasted no more time as he stood and scooped her up into his arms. She was so small that she felt as if she weighed nothing.

Jake held the back door open as he carried her toward the house.

"I wanted to tell her to come in, but Jake said I can't ever open the doors." Emily told him when he entered. She stood in the middle of the kitchen, then followed as Michael carried Tess back to the sofa.

"I'll call for an ambulance." Jake reached for the phone. Michael glanced at him. "No, wait a minute." He did another quick assessment of her physical condition. "Her pulse is strong and regular. She's breathing normally. Her cheeks have a bit more color. I think she's just cold. And sometimes her visions leave her so exhausted she faints. That may be all this is. Let's give her another minute."

He tucked the blanket around her and briskly rubbed one of Tess's hands in an effort to warm it. Then he moved to the other hand.

It seemed like forever before Tess's eyes fluttered open and she whispered hoarsely, "Michael . . ."

He met her gaze. "Geez, Tess, what are you trying to do, kill me slowly? Next time, just stick a knife in my chest. It would probably be quicker and easier to take."

"No . . . knives."

"Sorry. What the hell were you doing out there?"

"I had to see if I could control my connection with him. I had to see if I could find him and then come back on my own."

He let out a frustrated huff. "Damnit, Tess. You didn't have to do it this way. I could have at least been close-by where I could have helped you if you needed it. I could have been close enough that I could have kept you from kissing the grass and lying in the cold for God knows how long."

She closed her eyes and he watched her force a smile.

"Don't laugh," he groused. " I'm not joking. I'd like to shake some sense into you, but right now I'm more worried about getting you warm."

"You're squeezing my hand too hard."

"Sorry." He eased up on his death grip. "How long have you been out there? You're freezing. And I'm still not sure whether I want to hug you or shake some sense into you." He shook his head at her when she shook with silent laughter. "I mean it, stop laughing."

"I'm not laughing."

"That's because you're too busy shivering and clenching your teeth to keep them from chattering."

"I think she probably needs some bacon and eggs for

breakfast," Emily suddenly announced. "And hot chocolate will warm her up."

Emily's voice sounded different—more adult. Michael looked at Jake to find him staring at Emily with a startled expression, probably thinking the same thing.

"We'll make something in a few minutes, Emily." Jake's voice sounded tight and hesitant, as if he didn't know what to say to her.

Michael would have liked to delve further into Emily's sudden change, and he was certain Jake would, too. But right now anything new Tess might have learned was more important. "What happened, Tess? Did you connect with the guy?"

"Yes. I did it. I really did it on my own. And I did it without any help from the killer, too."

"How do you know?"

"Because he was sleeping, and he'd taken something to make himself sleep. When I finally did meet up with him, he faded in and out. One minute he was so incorporeal I could see through him, and the next he'd almost be solid, and his voice sounded like a radio with a faulty volume-control knob." She looked toward Jake. "I think it gets worse, Jake."

"How much worse?" Jake's voice sounded as if he forced air through closed vocal cords.

"He was hurt, bleeding. I think that's why he was fading in and out. He said he'd taken something for the pain. I don't know what happened to him, but there are only three women with him now."

Michael squeezed her hand as Jake closed his eyes and rubbed the bridge of his nose with his forefinger and thumb. "Do you have any idea where he is?"

Tess explained about the campground, the lake and the cabins, and she repeated everything that was said during her conversation with the killer.

"You never saw a name, not anything that would indicate what lake or which campground?" Jake asked. "Think again, Tess. You may have seen something—anything—that will give us a clue as to where to find this bastard"

"There was nothing, Jake. I tried to find something that would identify the place, but he stopped me before I could finish searching."

"I need to make you something warm to drink," Michael told her. "You're still pale and I can't seem to get your hands warm."

"I could make her something," Emily said. "Jake lets me use the microwave oven."

"Heat up a glass cup with water in it, Emily," Jake said told her.

"I know how to make hot chocolate, Jake." Emily moved off to do just that, and Jake stared after her for a long moment. Then he looked back at Tess. "You said the guy was bleeding. Did he tell you what happened? Do you think one of the women managed to hurt him?"

"I don't know," Tess said, her brow creased thoughtfully. Then she said, "Anna Carpelli. She's the one who was missing. He plans to kill the others today."

Jake let out an oath, then said, "He told you that?"

"Not exactly. I just know it's going to happen today."

Emily came in carrying a tray with four steaming mugs. "Here's the hot chocolate for all of us."

Jake looked at her. "Thank you."

"You're welcome, darling."

Michael watched as Jake stared at her with a shocked expression. "What did you call me?"

She placed the tray on the coffee table and frowned at him. "I called you darling, just like I always do. What's with you? You're staring at me as if you haven't seen me before."

"Um, sorry. I just . . . I . . . I've got to call Agents Black and Wheston. It would sure be helpful if you could come up with a few clues that could help us find him, Tess," he said as he dug his cell phone out of his pants pocket.

"I'm doing my best." Tess tried to sit up, and she stared at Emily, too. "But there just isn't much more I can tell you."

Michael reached out and cupped her cheek in the palm of his hand. "You said there was a marina. Did you see any signs?"

Tess met his gaze and then she tilted her head, as if she

was recalling something. "Yes," she said slowly. "I saw a neon sign right at the beginning when I first managed to go there. It was flashing, and I was trying to read it, but it was across the lake, pretty far away . . ." Her voice trailed off, and then she gasped. "It said something like The Happy Lander. But it could have said The Happy Landing."

"Now we're getting somewhere." Jake flipped open his phone, but it rang in before he could dial. He looked at the phone. "It's Agent Black. Maybe he has ESP," he teased as he hit the talk button. "Yes?" He paused and his hard gaze met Tess's. "Yes, I understand. We'll be there as soon as we can. We have information for you, too. And while we're on our way, you need to find out where The Happy Landing or The Happy Lander Marina is—he's in that area. And put a rush on it, Black. He's going to kill the remaining women today."

He flipped the phone closed and gave Tess and Michael a hard look. "Black and Wheston want us at the morgue. They found Anna Carpelli's body." His gaze softened as he looked at Emily. "Emily, I want you to get dressed. I know you don't normally come with me, but today maybe you should."

"Jake, I can't go with you. You know I'm working a seven to seven shift today. Besides, why would I want to go with you? I've never gone with you before."

He smiled and gently drew her into his arms. "I know, but I don't want to leave you alone right now and I need to see this through with Tess and Michael."

"I know, it's all right. Go do your job," Emily insisted. "I've got to go to work."

"Emily, your shift was cancelled. And I'm really afraid to leave you alone." He again flipped open his phone and dialed a speed number. "Yeah, Vitto, this is Jake. Can you come and stay with Emily for a while? I need to do something, and you need to be here." He paused, then said, "Thanks." He flipped the phone closed.

Emily drew close again and leaned her head on his shoulder. "Why are you calling my brother to come over? I don't need a baby sitter. And when was my shift cancelled? Was there a message on the machine that I didn't hear? Now that I think about it, I don't think I listened to the messages on the machine. I didn't make your cookies, either. Did I even stop and get another dozen eggs?"

Jake held her close. "Don't worry about it. You can make cookies later. Right now, I'm not sure what's going on, but I don't want you to be alone. And I can't stay." He looked over Emily's shoulder at Michael. "You can drive us, right?"

"Of course."

"Emily, we need to get dressed. I have to leave, and Vitto will be here in five minutes."

She giggled slightly. "Gosh, I didn't realize I was out here in just my nightgown. And where did I get this nightgown? Jake, I know this sounds stupid, but I feel like I just woke up from a really strange dream. Did Tess and Michael get here some time during the night?" She looked from Tess to Michael. "And I feel as if I know you—I mean I do know you, but I can't remember meeting you."

Jake let her go, but held her hand. "Come on. We have to get dressed, and we'll talk about everything later."

"I wish we had more time, I could fix Tess something to eat. I think you should hit a drive-thru on the way at least," Emily said.

Fifteen minutes later, Tess and Michael and Jake were in Michael's car, leaving Emily and Vitto at the kitchen table enjoying coffee. Tess held Michael's hand and worked to choke down a now-cooled cup of cocoa that had way too much sugar in it.

"I know I should be concentrating on this case, Tess, but I can't believe Emily is speaking so lucidly to me," Jake stated softly. "Not after two years of macaroni and cheese and chess."

"What are you going to do?" Tess asked.

"Take care of this bastard who's killing women so I can get my wife to the hospital for a CAT Scan and PET Scan. I'm calling her neurologist now. I'm sure Vitto will be want to take her to the hospital after listening to her for five minutes. I still can't believe this is happening."

Tess glanced into the backseat at Jake. He looked as if he might shake apart at any moment. "You should have stayed with her, Jake."

Michael squeezed Tess's hand. "We could go back and get her. Then I could drop you both off at the hospital right now. It's on our way."

"I don't think that's a good idea," Jake replied, his voice still tight with emotion. "You and Tess are supposed to stay with me."

"We'll be fine," Michael promised. "Wheston and Black are meeting us at the morgue, right? And we're going straight there. Nothing will happen. Don't worry about Tess and me. Just take care of your wife."

"As soon as I have you two safe with Wheston, I'll explain the situation and take Emily to the hospital. I'd sure like to be there to catch this guy, but this is just too important."

"We understand," Tess said.

"I just don't know what's happening. I'm afraid to be hopeful. But Dr. Sharp wants to see her as soon as possible. And after a few tests, we'll probably have more answers."

A short time later, they reached the morgue and met with Agents Black and Wheston. Jake quickly explained he had a family emergency, and Tess gave him a hug for good luck. "How will you get back since you rode with us?" she asked.

"Jake," Michael drew his attention before Jake could reply. "You can take my car."

"No, thanks anyway." Jake sounded as if his voice would crack at any moment. "I'll just take a cab. That way you guys aren't left stranded either."

"Let us know what happens," Tess made him promise.

He nodded. "I'll be in touch. I really do want to see this through with you, Tess."

"I know, but take care of Emily."

Within seconds, he was gone.

"What do you think of that?" Tess asked quietly as she and Michael made their way to the basement where the bodies were kept.

"Of what? Emily suddenly being herself again?"

"Yes. From a doctor's point of view."

"I think it's either a really good sign or really a bad sign. It probably means the bullet moved to a new part of her brain."

"Well, I hope it's a good sign." He gave her a huge smile, and she eyed him warily. "Why are you smiling at me like that?"

"You amaze me. You've been through hell all night, and we're in the morgue where you get to experience more of the same hell, and you're concerned about Emily."

She gave an embarrassed shrug before she leaned into his embrace and let the warmth of his arms give her some much-needed strength. "I know this sounds weird, but Emily is real and all my visions feel like make-believe. Emily's realness brings me a great deal of comfort in that chaotic, unpredictable make-believe world." She sighed against him. "What makes this so scary is I think it's almost over and I'm not sure I'll like the ending. With Emily, it may be a new beginning with some happiness."

"We can only hope." Michael was quiet as he held her. Then he asked, "Are you ready to go in?"

"Yes, I want to get this over with as quickly as possible." But as she left his embrace, she suddenly stopped and looked up at him. "Michael?"

"Yes?"

"Where will we go after this? I don't feel safe anywhere."

Michael gently touched her cheek with his fingertips. "Maybe you'll see a clue that will be enough to stop this guy, and it will be over and we can go home."

"That sounds wonderful."

She leaned into his hand, and Michael thought her skin was softer than silk. "Does it matter which home we go to?" he had to ask. "Yours or mine?"

He sighed silently as she shook her head.

"Will you hold my hand?" she asked.

"Every second," he promised.

She pushed her way into the cooler. Michael kept his hand on her back, not wanting to stop touching her for a second. And a moment later, they stood together, a sheet-clad body lay on the slab before them.

Tess squeezed Michael's hand, not quite ready to let go of

him. "So what do you think about Black and Wheston being miffed about the fact that I said I wouldn't try to get a vision from this victim if they came in here with me? Do you think I did the right thing?"

"I think they'll get over it. And I think you need to do this your way," Michael replied softly. "But I'll bet they're bothered more by the fact that their colleagues haven't found The Happy Landing or Lander Marina yet. Let me know when you're ready."

"Do you know why I told them no audience?"

"No, why?"

"They'd be pushy. They'd be pacing like caged panthers, waiting impatiently. You never push me, Michael. Every time I've ever come in here, you're right beside me, letting me take my time. I think that's why the visions are so clear when I'm here with you."

Michael leaned close to her. "I learned long ago that the dead have a great deal to tell if one is patient enough to listen. I'm going to pull down the sheet now."

She drew in a calming breath. "All right."

Any calm she'd mustered was shattered when he pulled the sheet down. Anna Carpelli's face was battered and bruised, and her spiked, blond hair was matted with dried blood.

Tess leaned against him suddenly. She listened to the strong beat of his heart and tried to gain strength. "Oh, Michael, I don't know if I can do this again. I'm suddenly afraid, so terribly afraid. I feel like this killer has somehow slipped under my skin and I can't get him out, much less walk away without taking a part of him with me."

"It's all right, Tess. If you don't want to do this again, then don't. We'll just walk out of here and tell Black and Wheston that you saw nothing when you took her hand."

She looked up at him in disbelief. "You'd do that for me? You'd lie to them?"

"Yep, without hesitation."

"But he's a killer. He needs to be stopped."

"Then the cops will have to find another way to stop him. You're just as important to me, and this is taking its toll on you.

Hell, you haven't eaten properly since I made you my world-famous breakfast, and you haven't had a decent night's sleep since all of this started. The dark circles under your eyes tell how hard this is on you. If you need to give it a break, then give it a break. We could even head south to some warmer temperatures for a few days, if you want."

The offer touched her heart like a warm ray of sunshine. "That sounds wonderful."

"We could lay on the beach," Michael whispered in her ear. "Naked. So don't worry about wasting any time packing clothes." She smiled and relaxed against him as he added, "We could make love in the sand, in the sun as well as in the moonlight, with the waves crashing around us."

"Can we leave now?"

With one finger, he tilted her chin up until she looked at him. Then he gently brushed his lips against hers. "Whenever you want."

She slipped out of his arms and turned to face the body. Michael let her go. He knew she'd never turn her back on this job until the killer was caught, but he'd also known she'd needed his reassurance that if she did want to leave, he'd take her. And he hadn't been lying. He'd have run off with her in a heartbeat, if that was what she wanted.

He watched as she studied Anna Carpelli, and he could tell by her intense expression that she was preparing herself for the ordeal that would come the moment she touched the woman.

"I'll be right here with you," he assured her.

She nodded, swallowed hard and took a heavy breath. Then she reached out and grasped Anna Carpelli's cold hand.

* * * *

It was difficult not to struggle. It was equally difficult to lie still and pretend to be limp and drugged. Since leaving the house where Raymond had killed her two childhood friends, he'd kept her and the two others drugged by stuffing pills down them regularly. Well, she'd managed to cough up the previous dose while he'd drugged one of the others, and this time, she'd held the pill in her mouth so long she feared she'd still feel the effects of the drug. But after administering his "medication," he jumped out the back of the van, slammed the door and moved toward the driver's door. She took the opportunity to spit out the pill. Now, all she had to do was close her eyes, breathe evenly, as if she really slept, and gather her strength and wait for the right moment. He wasn't any taller that she was, and he seemed as clumsy as an ox. Thank heavens, he thought his drug was enough to keep them subdued, and he only had their wrists tied, not their feet. Otherwise, she would really be limited in her actions. One kick to the knee—she noticed he had a slight limp on the left, so she'd aim for that knee. Then she'd kick him in the solar plexus hard enough to knock him off his feet. Hopefully, he'd land on his back, which he'd broken when he'd fallen off the cliff all those years ago. When he was down, she thought a kick to his face would be best. With luck, he'd lose consciousness for a few hours. And with the way he'd bound her wrists together, she planned to lace her fingers and hit him as hard as she could with one big fist. The last week had shown her more than once there was no bargaining with the man. It had also proved that he meant to kill her.

Well, she was not about to go down without a fight, and with the element of surprise on her side, she should be able to whip Raymond Bradford enough to escape. But what would happen to the other three once she took off? She was sure he'd take his anger out on them, and since they were out cold, they couldn't do anything to defend themselves. That was why she had to kick him in the head hard enough to knock him out. Then she'd leave him lying on the road and drive the other three women to safety.

The sound of the wheels on the pavement nearly lulled her to sleep, but she concentrated her thoughts on her husband and her kids to stay awake. Soon she'd be home with them. She wasn't sure how much time passed before the pavement changed to what sounded like gravel. The van turned sharply and she allowed herself to roll with it as her three sleeping companions did.

A few moments later, the van stopped, and Raymond climbed out. Then she heard footsteps crunching on gravel and the back door opened.

She tried to watch him through half-closed eyes. She tried to make out her surroundings. It was night, and there was little light from the moon. Was that some sort of a screened cabin or hut behind him?

He pulled out one of the other three women and heaved her over his shoulder like a sack of potatoes. When he turned and moved away, she opened her eyes. Yes, that was a cabin with nothing more than a screened door that he pulled open. It slammed shut with an echoing thud after he passed through the doorway. She heard a thump, and she assumed he'd deposited his burden onto something. A moment later, he returned. Again, the door closed with a thud.

She quickly closed her eyes and forced her breathing and her heartbeat to slow as she mulled over what she'd seen. They had to be miles away from any place they could be seen because he didn't seem the least bit worried about the sound made by the slamming cabin door. She cracked her eyes open as he slid her second companion from the van and hefted her onto his shoulders, just as he had the previous one.

Because she was closer than the fourth woman in the van, she knew she would be next. As she waited for his return, she breathed deeply once, twice, three times, working to gain her strength. She'd gone so long without food. And except for the small bit of water to wash down the pills he'd forced on her, she hadn't had anything to drink. Her mouth was dry, her lips cracked and painful.

She closed her eyes. She didn't need to watch him return; she felt him. She sensed him. She knew he was close even before he grasped her ankles and pulled her toward the back of the van. Her heart pounded in her chest. What if he felt it? She held her breath and worked to stay limp and relaxed, to not give away that she was awake.

When he released her ankles, she didn't hesitate. She reared back and kicked him with both heels at the same time. Her right heel made contact with his chin, her left the top of his chest. Her kick sent him sprawling backwards, but didn't knock him off his feet.

She jumped out of the van, so pumped up on adrenaline that her weak legs barely wobbled when her feet hit the ground. She didn't bother with aiming for a knee as she'd planned. Her idea was just to kick hard and fast. She raised her leg and kicked him again, square in the chest. This time, her kick knocked him too the ground, and he lay there gasping for breath.

Forget about that fair fight idea of never kicking a man when he's down, she thought, and kicked him in the face. She thought she felt a few teeth break off. His cry of pain echoed through the foggy darkness. Next, she stomped on his knee the one she'd first planned to kick. He cried out again, sounding almost like a girl.

"You brought us back to the Little Creek Campground? What'd you think? That you could push us all off the same bluff? Bastard!"

Suddenly, he pulled out his knife, and she knew she never should have paused, should never have taken the time to utter a word. She had completely forgotten how he had slipped the knife into his pocket after killing Jill. She had also forgotten that even though he walked with a limp and moved clumsily, he used the knife with unbelievable speed. When she moved to kick him again, he managed to grasp her foot. She hardly saw him move as he slashed her leg with it.

It was her turn to scream as his blade sliced through skin and muscle, and through her Achilles' tendon before it stopped at the bone of her heel.

Pain—white and hot—caused her vision to blur and moved up through her body like fire all the way to the top of her head. Worse than childbirth, worse than sticking her hand in hot grease, worse than anything she could imagine, the pain swirled through her and grew in its heated intensity.

She screamed again, didn't realize she was falling, until the unforgiving ground suddenly met her chin. More hot pain coursed through her as the cold steel penetrated her leg just above her knee.

He was up on all fours then, and she couldn't see past her agony to stop him or move away. The warm stickiness of her blood cooled in the night air. The copper smell of it touched her nose and her stomach heaved.

Damnit! She couldn't let him win. She refused to die on her knees. She used her elbow to hit him in the face. Hell, it hurt to move. Her elbow hurt now, too, but she had to survive.

Blood spurted from his nose and he dropped the knife to cup his face. She didn't hesitate. She grabbed the knife and ignored the fresh wave of pain as she grabbed the blade by mistake and cut her fingers. But she managed to twist the knife around and again didn't hesitate as she slipped the blade into his side.

The oath he let out was quickly lost in the night. She gave the blade a twist and looked down, relishing in the blood she saw pour from his wound.

She should have never taken her gaze from him. If she hadn't, she might have seen his fist coming toward her face, might have been able to duck out of the way.

Pain exploded in her head as his fist connected with it. The impact knocked her to the ground, knocked the wind out of her. The pain in her leg was unbearable, unimaginable, like a great wall she couldn't climb.

His knife reflected what little light the moon cast. It was merely a flash before she felt it stab into her chest and her neck.

Then she felt nothing at all.

* * * *

Tess opened her eyes to find Michael standing before her, holding her arms, keeping her on her feet. She stared up at him for a long moment before he came into complete focus.

"A place called the Little Creek Campground." Tess forced the words out in a hoarse whisper and each utterance hurt her throat. "That's where he has the last three—in a cabin at the Little Creek Campground. Cabin number thirteen."

She looked beyond Michael to the door before she leaned against him, exhausted. Agents Black and Wheston stood there, and Black said, "We're taking a team and heading there now. And we have the name of a man who matches the description and spent some time in a coma after a fall at camp. His name is Raymond . . ."

"Bradford," Tess supplied. "Anna Carpelli called him Raymond Bradford."

It was clear by Wheston's hesitation and the look on his face that he had watched her ability at work and would rather have pulled out his notebook and asked her a few questions.

Michael held Tess tighter in his arms. "I'm going to take Tess home, feed her a hot meal and let her rest."

Wheston cleared his throat. "That's probably a good idea. We'll call Detective Williams and let him know what's going on, too."

He left the room. It was Agent Black who hesitated to leave. "Thank you, Tess."

Still resting against Michael's chest, she merely nodded. A moment later, Tess and Michael were alone in the room. Well, not quite alone, but they didn't need to worry about anyone overhearing any conversation. None of the people on the gurnies were going to listen.

Tess drew in a deep breath and merely continued to lean against Michael, relishing in the strong, steady beat of his heart, as he asked, "Are you all right?"

Tess tightened her hold on him. "I don't know. It's kind of hard to tell right now. He stabbed her out of anger," Tess whispered. "She almost got the better of him." She leaned against him and breathed in the clean smell of him in an effort to stop the tears that instantly came to her eyes.

Without hesitation, he swallowed her in his embrace.

A few moments later, with his arm wound around her tightly, Michael led Tess from the cool room, through the building and outside into the equally cool morning sunlight.

In the car, he held her hand as they waited for the heater to kick in, and said, "I know where the Little Creek Campground is. I went there as a kid a few times. Black and Wheston will be there in no time, so I guess we can relax. This mess is about over."

Tess looked up at him and bleakly said, "He still has three women he can kill."

Chapter Fifteen

At the hospital, Jake gripped the arms of his chair, feeling like a man on a wild, out-of-control roller coaster as he waited for Emily's test results. He hadn't been allowed to stay with her, and her confusion pushed against his heart even as hope pushed it from the other direction. Could she be better? Could the bullet have moved to a place in her brain that no longer affected her? Or was her sudden lucidity, combined with the increased zone-out times she'd been experiencing, merely a nearing of the end?

He swallowed and his throat was painfully dry. He should call Markus Black and see what was going on with the case. He should also call Michael and Tess and make sure they were still safe. He should make both calls, but he didn't reach for his phone. The edges of the chair arms bit into his fingers. He forced in a breath. His lungs burned. His throat burned. The tiles on the floor blurred together for a moment.

Then, without warning, Loafers moved into his line of vision. "Mr. Williams?"

Jake let his gaze move slowly up, past the gray trousers, white shirt, white lab coat and dark tie, to meet Dr. Sharp's gaze. It was an ironic, almost funny, name for one of the greatest neurosurgeons in the country, Jake thought. He didn't speak to the doctor because he wasn't certain what might come out—a scream, a cry, begging? Or worse, he might start crying. So he just looked up as he continued to force in breath after breath.

Dr. Sharp didn't speak either as he sat down beside him.

"This is the end, isn't it?" Jake finally said. "It's like rabies, right? She'll be lucid and coherent for a day or two before her heart stops." Jake squeezed his eyes shut for a long moment in hopes that when he opened them again, he'd find this was all a terrible nightmare.

Dr. Sharp cleared his throat, and Jake sucked in another deep breath as he tried to prepare for the worst. The breath didn't help. Maybe he should ask for some oxygen. He was, after all, in a hospital. Oxygen was readily available.

"I don't think so," Dr. Sharp said softly.

"What?" He turned toward the doctor so quickly, he heard his neck pop.

"I don't want to raise false hopes," the doctor said, but it appears from the scan and the X-ray that the bullet is moving away from the center of the brain. If it continues moving, it will go to her temple, above her right ear, where we'll be able to remove it."

Jake let out his breath, feeling as if he'd been holding it for the last five minutes. "What does this mean?"

Dr. Sharp's hand gripped his arm. "I don't know for certain, Jake. Right now, she's back to normal. She remembers her job, her life and you—everything her life was before she was shot. She remembers very little of the past two years, however. Other than this sudden reversal, has anything else unusual happened with her?"

Jake shrugged. "Other than the zone-outs, no." Then he frowned. "That's not exactly true. She knew Tess and Michael, two people who were at our house, even though she hadn't met them before the shooting. And she really did know them, even though there was no way she could. Don't you think that's odd?"

Dr. Sharp shook his head. "When it comes to the brain, there are a lot of 'odd' things, particularly when there's been brain trauma, that can't always be explained. The brain is a very complex machine. I can say, however, that at this point, it's possible that Emily will have a nearly complete recovery."

"When can I take her home? Her family will want to see her." Jake said, although he wasn't sure he was ready to share her with anyone else just yet. He wanted to just take her home and hold her in his arms until next week. Even then, that might not be long enough. He gripped the chair again to keep from jumping to his feet and kissing Dr. Sharp on both cheeks and then running down the hall, jumping up and down and whooping at the top of his lungs.

"You can take her home right now. I'll go tell the staff to release her."

With his heart so overjoyed that it felt as if it might pop out the front of his chest, Jake couldn't remember if he'd even said thank you to the wonderful Dr. Sharp as he watched the man disappear through a nearby pair of swinging doors.

A moment later, Emily suddenly stood before him, but she seemed more bewildered than ever as she looked around the waiting room and then back at Jake. "It really has been two years, hasn't it? The hospital looks different somehow, and yet it doesn't. Does that make any sense? I mean I don't know anybody here, and my head doesn't even hurt. So why can't I remember?"

Jake pulled himself to his feet and took her in his arms. "Don't worry, my love. Please, don't worry. Just let me hold you. You don't have to worry about anything."

She pulled away from him slightly. "But we do have to worry. About Tess. We should never have left Tess."

Jake looked down at her, his heart pounding again, but this time in worry. "What about Tess?"

"She's in danger, Jake. Really bad danger."

* * * *

Michael carried the drive-thru sacks that held some much-needed breakfast and followed Tess through her front door. "You're hesitant."

"This doesn't feel like my house anymore, not like it did. I feel like he managed to worm his way in and make it dirty, even though all he really did was put flowers on the front porch. And then the guys in black suits came in here and finished the job for him," she said, as they stepped into the living room.

"Well, I put off bringing you here for you as long as I could," Michael said. "I kept you at the morgue until I thought you'd fall asleep on your feet. Then I took the long way back so you could watch the sun rise over the lake. Then I drove through a drive-thru and picked you up a ninety-nine cent heart attack in a bag—well, it was more like a dollar and ninety-nine cents."

Tess smiled at his joke.

He smiled back. " I see what you're really trying to do, you know."

"What's that?" she asked innocently.

"You're putting off eating so this wonderful breakfast can get cold. Then you'll tell me you can't eat it at all."

"Oh, you read me so well. The truth is, after experiencing your fantastic breakfast, no other can live up to it, certainly not this." She took the bag from him, held it up and then deposited it on the coffee table. Then Tess sniffed, detecting an odd odor, as if something had died, but she couldn't locate where the smell came from. "I guess it's not really so bad in here. Maybe."

"Well, if you're not completely comfortable, you can pack another bag, open all the windows and stay with me while the place airs out," Michael offered. "Or if you don't want to stay here long enough to pack, I can take you to my place and just make you breakfast."

"That sounds so nice, but I can't believe how tired I am. I'm not sure I can walk another step. And I have a headache that just won't go away." She dropped onto the couch and closed her eyes.

"You didn't get much rest last night. And do you have anything for your headache? I'll get it for you."

"It was packed in my bag."

"Oh, your bag is still out in my trunk." He stepped closer and gently fingered her hair before brushing his fingertips across her cheeks. She didn't open her eyes. "Just rest. I'll go get it, and I'll be right back. You can take something for your headache, and we can eat this great take-out. Or if you don't want it, I can see what I can find in your kitchen to make for you. You can rest. Then I can make you my world-famous lunch."

"That sounds like a plan. Maybe I'll feel better after I eat something."

Michael's fingers lingered for another long moment as he wondered if he could coax her to shower with him and then they could sleep together, locked in one another's arms. But first things first. He'd get her bag so she could get rid of her headache and then he'd feed her. Gently, he leaned down and touched his lips to hers before he headed for the door.

Outside, the air was warmer than that of the previous rainy day. He looked up and thought that perhaps the sun might win the battle with the clouds today. He and Tess might get to finally enjoy a picnic. He'd sure like to kiss her in the sunshine.

He smiled at the thought and stepped off the porch, walking to his car at the curb. A neighbor drove past and waved as Michael opened the trunk. Nice neighborhood, he thought. And it hurt to know that a maniac had made Tess feel uncomfortable in her home, the one place where she should feel safe. He hoped it wasn't a permanent problem. He knew very well how ghosts could haunt a person's home.

After he pulled her bag from the trunk, he looked around again and took note of the breaking day.

He took the four steps to her porch in two of his own. But when he reached the front door, he noticed it was closed. He frowned at it. He didn't remember closing it. Then he reached out and turned the handle.

The door was locked.

* * * *

Tess liked what she saw from the inside of her eyelids. Fatigue had hit her like a Mack truck—sudden and hard and equally unforgiving. True, the visions and her jump to the campground had left her exhausted, but her energy had been easily restored with a drink of tea and a bit of sugar. This fatigue was overwhelming, probably from days of little sleep and few meals to provide fuel. And Michael had been right. She no longer wanted her breakfast from a bag.

Without opening her eyes, she kicked off her shoes and pulled her feet up onto the sofa. The only things missing were Michael's warm, hard body and a cozy afghan. But the former would soon be remedied, she thought, as she heard the dull thud as he closed the trunk of his car. It would be only a matter of seconds before he was close again.

She felt herself begin to drift in that netherworld between wakefulness ad sleep, when Michael touched her. It was sooner than she'd expected. She hadn't even heard the front door open or close.

The warmth of his hand on her cheek was subtle and hesitant. Knowing he was being careful not to startle her, she smiled and reached up to place her hand over his.

His fingers warm and sticky with wetness.

"What the . . .?" she began as she opened her eyes—and looked up into Raymond Bradford's face.

His blood-covered hand still rested lightly on her cheek. And in his other hand, he held his knife.

The same knife he'd used to kill so many others.

Chapter Sixteen

Whose blood was that on Raymond Bradford's hands? Michael's?

Just the thought made her want to scream Michael's name, to leap from the sofa and go looking for him.

Instead, she forced herself to calm down. If Michael was hurt, she couldn't help him if she was injured herself. Somehow, she had to get away from this madman in one piece, and she had to do it quickly. If Michael was lying somewhere bleeding . . .

She cut off the thought. Thinking about Michael wouldn't help right now. Instead, she focused her complete attention on the man in front of her. He was pale and the knife in his hand was not quite steady. She wanted to look at his side to see if he was still bleeding from wound she'd seen in her vision, but she was afraid to break eye contact with him.

"Why are you looking at me like that?" she asked him, fighting to keep her voice even. The last thing she wanted was for him hear her terror.

"I still can't believe you're real," he said, his voice filled with an odd mixture of confusion and curiosity. "All this time, I thought you were a dream. Even when I came here and left the flowers on your porch, I expected to find someone else living here, just like the woman in Oak Park was the wrong woman." He sat down beside her and held the knife where he could, no doubt, use it quickly. "How did you do it, anyway?"

"Do what?"

"Get into my house, my van, and my campground."

"It took a lot of concentration." Tess replied.

"I'll bet."

Michael chose that moment to beat on the front door, screaming, "Tess!"

Tess turned sharply toward the foyer and the front door. Thank God, Michael was all right. So whose blood was on the knife?

She risked a glance down and saw that the man was still bleeding from the knife wound Anna Carpelli had given him. No wonder he looked so pale. Anna had stabbed him hours ago. He had to have lost a lot of blood.

Before she could analyze what that might mean, he suddenly held the knife to her throat. "Tell him to leave now and I'll let him live."

Tess didn't believe him. But whether it was true or not, she couldn't put Michael in danger when she had the opportunity keep him safe, even if it was only for a short time.

"Let me go closer to the door so he can hear me," she said. "Otherwise, he probably won't believe me."

"If you try anything stupid, it will be the last thing you do."

"I understand. I won't try anything." Although the urge to try *something* was nearly overpowering. He was bleeding and in pain. She might win if she tried to overpower him. Then she thought of Anna Carpelli, and she was terrified to take the chance.

She rose from the sofa, and as they moved closer to the door, he held her close to him, keeping the knife blade against her skin. Tess took small, controlled breaths, but she couldn't slow her racing heart. Nor could she keep out his smell—sweat, blood and that underlying greasy, locker room smell that caused her stomach to roll.

"Tess! What the hell is going on?" Michael's voice came through the door loud and clear.

"I changed my mind, Michael. I want to be alone. Why don't you just go home, and I'll call you later." Even to her own ears, her words sounded phony, even out of character.

"What?" The disbelief in that single word oozed through the door like mist. "Come on, Tess. Let me in."

The knifepoint poked the tender skin of her neck, and she tried again. "No, really," she said, although it was nearly impossible to force out the words with her heart pounding and her throat so constricted it felt as if she were choking. "I just want to be alone. I'm really tired."

"Tess, what's going on?" Now it was confusion in his voice.

"Nothing, I just need some space. Things between us are

happening too fast."

There was a long pause. Then finally, "All right if that's what you really want. I'll leave your bag here on the porch."

"Thank you. I'll get it later."

She thought it odd that he never said good-bye or see you later or even go to hell. There was simply silence. Then again, she'd just told him to leave, so he was probably angry.

Raymond suddenly shoved her around and pressed her back against the front door. Once again, he held the knife at her throat. "I should kill you right here, right now."

"Why?" she forced out.

"Why? You need to ask?"

"Yes." She tried to keep calm, but she didn't think her legs would have held her up if he wasn't pinning her to the door.

"Because you ruined all of my plans!" His spittle sprayed her face as he shouted, and she didn't dare move to wipe it away.

"I did?"

"Oh, you are a real trip, lady," he said. "Of course you did. You ran me out of my house before I was ready to leave. And after you showed up there, all my well-made plans fell apart. The women became unruly, forcing me to kill them sooner than I planned. Then you showed up in my van, probably managed to even tell the cops where I was. After that I could barely drive. I kept expecting to see you at any minute. When I finally get my girls to the camp and feel my plans might just come together, there you are again. I couldn't do a damned thing without you intruding. Every time I turned around, there you were!"

She decided not to tell him that she couldn't have done any of those things without his help, that the time he'd spent in a coma had somehow linked them. Instead, she simply stared up at him.

Again, she thought about trying to escape. He was, after all, injured. But then he slowly moved the knife down the front of her body, and she recalled how fast he'd been with the knife when he'd killed Anna Carpelli, and that was after she'd injured him.

He reached out and touched her face. "I really should kill you and get the hell out of here, but I'm still not sure you're real. Have you just popped in here like you did all the other places?"

Suddenly, from behind Raymond, a deep, male voice commanded, "Put the knife down, Bradford."

Tess didn't have to see Agent Markus Black to recognize his voice, and she didn't dare take her gaze from the killer or the knife he held.

Raymond's mouth twisted into a lopsided grin as he stared down at Tess. He seemed as unwilling to look away from her as she was from him. "You won't shoot at me. You might miss and hit her."

"Please risk it, Agent Black," Tess said, working hard to keep her voice from shaking.

"I'll risk it if he won't." Tess recognized Jake's voice from her left. He must be standing in her bedroom doorway.

The killer chuckled. "Neither of you will risk it."

The knife came crashing toward her, and Tess stared at it, managing to jerk out of the way at the last moment. With a thud, the knife point sank into the solid oak of her front door at the same time that two shots rang through the house and seemed to echo off the walls.

Raymond fell against her, once again pinning her against the door. His knife was still embedded in the wood, but as he slowly slid down the door to the floor, he somehow managed to take it with him.

Tess stared down at him, unable to move away. She didn't know whether to scream or to cry or to faint dead away. Then Michael was there, and he pulled her to safety, away from the killer and his knife.

He held her for a long moment, and when Tess finally found the strength to look back at the killer who had terrorized her dreams, she found his gaze fixed and lifeless, staring at nothing.

Still, Agent Markus Black kicked the knife that had been used to kill so many people out of reach.

"What about the other three women?" Tess asked, almost

afraid to hear the answer.

She sagged in relief when Markus said, "They're drugged, but we found them at the campground, in cabin thirteen, just like you said. I'm sure they're at the hospital by now and their families are being notified." Markus slipped his gun back into his holster as Jake joined them.

Jake eyed Raymond Bradford, then told Markus, "It was my bullet that killed him."

Markus gave him a bored look. "No, I fired first."

Tess nearly laughed. "It doesn't matter, gentlemen. You both saved my life, and thank you. Besides, I'm sure both of you have days of paperwork about this investigation ahead of you."

Jake turned and met Tess's gaze. "Are you all right?"

"Yes. How's Emily?"

"Fine. I still can't believe it. She's better. She's herself. The doctor thinks he may even be able to remove the bullet. She's out in the car. She insisted she come with me." He glanced at Markus. "Maybe I will let you have all the glory so I can take my wife home and spend some much-needed time with her."

Markus shrugged, as if he didn't care either way. Then he looked at Tess. "You're sure you're okay?"

"I think so." She smiled at him and said, "We saved those three women. It was all worth it because we saved them."

He returned her smile. "You saved them. We might never have found them without you. Thank you."

"You're welcome."

She turned and looked up at Michael.

Michael searched her gaze, as if he looked for something in particular. Then he said, "You've been so connected to him. Do you feel anything now that he's dead? Did you feel his pain when he was shot?"

Tess looked at the dead man on the floor. "No, I feel nothing." Then she met Michael's gaze. "Can we go to your house now?"

"Honey, we'll go anywhere you want."

A moment later, Michael led Tess out into the morning

sunshine where she took his hand and stopped him.

"Didn't you promise me a picnic?" she asked.

"I think I also said we could spend time being naked on the beach. Which would you prefer?"

He silenced her chuckle with a kiss.

Epilogue

The sun was warm. Tess looked up, soaking in the sunshine like a sponge soaks in water, allowing the golden orb's warmth to touch her soul. She let out a long, contented sigh, and Michael pulled her closer until she leaned against him. Remnants of sandwiches and potato salad on paper plates and sparkling apple juice in plastic champagne goblets littered the blanket beside them.

"This is wonderful," she murmured.

"Yes, it is," he agreed. "Just took a bit longer than I anticipated to finally get our picnic."

She smiled up at him. "That's true."

He studied her face. "What are you thinking?"

"What a terrible thing peer pressure is."

"Oh?"

Tess snuggled closer to him. "I think of how Raymond Bradford was treated all through his teenage years—never invited anywhere, always laughed at, not much different from the way I was treated. He and Mary fell off that cliff ledge before anyone could even think to help them, and because he'd always been treated so callously, it was easy for him to blame all those women, to hate them. It's really kind of sad when you think about it in those terms."

"Yes, it is sad, but why are you thinking about him now?"

She shrugged. "I don't know. I guess because I'm feeling so happy, so content, I was looking back at my life, and I realized I spent a long time blaming and hating people for the way I was treated. In many ways, I was just like Raymond Bradford."

Michael took her hand and gave it a squeeze. "Don't compare yourself to him. You never killed anyone or even planned to, for that matter."

"I know. But why did I turn out so differently?"

"I don't know, Tess. I'm just glad you did. And I'm really

glad you haven't connected to anyone else since."

"Oh, me, too."

"Are you sure about tonight?"

She rolled her eyes at him. "How many times are you going to ask me this?"

"I just don't want you to have any second thoughts, and if you do, now is the time to share them."

Tess looked away, her gaze growing distant as she watched Jake and Emily flying a kite. "Are you having second thoughts?" she had to ask.

"No," he replied without hesitation.

"What if I connect to someone or have even stranger visions?"

He reached out and took her hand. "I'll be there, holding your hand."

She smiled then turned her attention back to Jake and Emily. "They look happy, don't they?"

Michael smiled. "They are happy, like we are, like I want us to be forever. So . . ."

She punched him lightly on the arm, and he pretended to be hurt, letting out an, "Ouch!"

"I'm happy; you're happy. We've determined that I don't have nightmares or walk in my sleep or do anything else that will keep you awake—well, nothing that you wouldn't want to keep you awake," she amended with a grin. "So, yes, I still plan to move in with you tonight. And before you ask again, no, I haven't changed my mind about the ring you gave me, and, yes, I'm putting my house on the market before the end of the week. But there is just one thing—"

"What?" he sounded alarmed, and she almost burst into laughter.

"I've always wanted to be married on the beach, in the sun, barefooted. Would that bother you?"

He grinned. "Would it bother you if all my brothers and sisters and the rest of the family were there, all barefooted, too?"

"No, but . . ."

"But what?"

She offered him a grin. "You promised we could be naked on the beach, too. They'll have to leave for that part."

He grinned back at her. "We might have to bribe them, but it can be done." He leaned close and kissed her warmly on the mouth. "When would you like to get married?"

Tess had to think for a long moment. "I could see if my brother's free for Thanksgiving."

"Nope, it can't be Thanksgiving."

"Why not?" Tess asked.

"I already told everyone we'd have Thanksgiving dinner."

"You did what? When were you going to tell me about this?" She wanted to be angry, but found when it came to Michael, it was impossible.

He shrugged lightly. "I figured I'd tell you as soon as you came up with a wedding date."

"Okay, we can do Thanksgiving, but you're making the pies," she insisted. "I hate rolling out the crust."

He chuckled. "I buy the packaged stuff." He looked down and kissed her again. "So what date can we tell our families— the week before Thanksgiving?"

"That sounds wonderful. I have a lot to be thankful for— starting with you."

"So you'll marry me for sure?"

"Absolutely."

She sealed her promise with a kiss.

CPSIA information can be obtained at www.ICGtesting.com
Printed in the USA
BVOW071848170512

290489BV00001B/70/P